KV-387-646

LV 19017227

Liverpool Libraries

STRAWBERRY ROAN

STRAWBERRY ROAN

Nelson Nye

Chivers Press • **Thorndike Press**
Bath, England **Waterville, Maine USA**

This Large Print edition is published by Chivers Press, England, and by Thorndike Press, USA.

Published in 2002 in the U.K. by arrangement with the author c/o Golden West Literary Agency.

Published in 2002 in the U.S. by arrangement with Golden West Literary Agency.

U.K. Hardcover ISBN 0–7540–7450–1 (Chivers Large Print)
U.K. Softcover   ISBN 0–7540–7451–X (Camden Large Print)
U.S. Softcover   ISBN 0–7862–4487–9 (Nightingale Series Edition)

Copyright © 1953 by Nelson Nye
Copyright © 1964, 1969 by Nelson Nye
Copyright © renewed 1981 by Nelson Nye

All rights reserved.

The text of this Large Print edition is unabridged.
Other aspects of the book may vary from the original edition.

Set in 16 pt. New Times Roman.

Printed in Great Britain on acid-free paper.

British Library Cataloguing in Publication Data available

Library of Congress Cataloging-in-Publication Data

Nye, Nelson C. (Nelson Coral), 1907–
    Strawberry roan / Nelson Nye.
        p. cm.
    ISBN 0–7862–4487–9 (lg. print : sc : alk. paper)
    1. Ranch life—Fiction. 2. Large type books. I. Title.
PS3527.Y33 S8 2002
813'.54—dc21   2002020487

CHIV 28 · 2 · 03

LIBRARY & INFORMATION

CHAPTER ONE

When Morgan Price first saw the woman she was being helped aboard by the talkative driver who seemed as handy with lies as he was with the ribbons. Not seeing her face, and being taken up with prospects likely to prove more important than the look of an ankle, he promptly forgot her.

Ignoring the wind, the clomp and clank of shod hoofs and the loquacious Hi Henry, who spat, cracked his whip and occasionally cursed without noticeable interruption to his interminable stories, Price, who'd climbed onto the box last night at Duncan, sat wrapped in his thoughts of the morrow's meeting and the possible results of a regretted impulse.

Good jobs were scarce in this man's country and, when the notion had hit him, punching cattle for thirty a month had seemed like a mighty slow way of acquiring his iron and a secure independence.

The knock can usually be heard if a man will listen, and Price had figured to have caught it when he had torn out and answered that ad he'd come across in the Signal City paper. And so for forty-three wheel-grinding bone-jolting miles he had ridden with the vision of imagined prosperity. That little spread of his own had seemed a pretty near thing.

1

It wasn't until the stage pulled into Solomonsville for a shift to fresh horses—and a bite for such passengers as didn't mind the look of Holy Joe's grub—that Price began subconsciously to scan the back of this picture. He was not so sure then but that he'd done a crazy thing in pitching up that job he'd had with Two Pole Pumpkin.

Hunching broad shoulders against the station's lit front, hardly hearing the gab and chatter coming through the torn screen, he dug the much-thumbed ad from out of a vest pocket. He knew every word by heart but took another squint at it.

WANTED: Ranch manager—one who can't be bluffed—or backed down. Generous pay to right party. E. D. Sloan, Box 4, Signal City Star.

His first reaction very probably had been the only sane one he had had since he'd latched onto it. With a snort of disgust he'd flung the paper away. 'Sucker bait!' he'd muttered. But later, when the rest of the boys had been pounding their ears, he'd got to thinking how long it would take to build a spread up on three-sixty a year and that *can't be bluffed or backed down* had looked a whole lot better. He'd hunted the paper out again and written Sloan offering his services.

He hadn't really expected ever to hear from

2

the fellow but Sloan's answer when it came, in a surprisingly legible hand, had all but set him back on his haunches.

One hundred and fifty cartwheels a month the guy had promised; and the tone of his epistle showed he expected Price to earn it. He wanted to be met in the Orrison Hotel at Sunflower on the 5th (which was tomorrow) for a discussion of 'relevant details' and 'inasmuch as your stipend is being computed from the 1st, I'll expect you to be there as specified,' Sloan had said.

The more Price rolled it around the less he liked it. The guy wasn't putting up dough like that for Price to tell a crew where and when to chouse cattle.

Thirty a month might be slow but it was regularly sure, and the only sure thing he could dig from Sloan's letter was an imminence of disaster. There was a queer fishy smell about this whole deal. The only one of his questions Sloan had bothered to answer was the one about wage, and operating cow spreads didn't pay that kind of money.

Price's blunt fingers shredded the clipping and a low ground breeze farmed the fluttering fragments over against the dirt wall of the horse barns. Price's long lips pressed thinly together. He had searched out by now the primary source of his unease, the thing which had finally fetched his thoughts from the engaging fancies induced by Sloan's

3

preposterous offer.

Sunflower.

A mirthless grin crossed Price's mouth and he pitched away his smoke. He'd been to Sunflower once to buy some heifers for the Pumpkin and every detail of that trip still lay indelibly in his head. He squared broad shoulders and followed Hi Henry across the hoof-tracked dust, a big-boned man with the distributed weight of a cougar. Tousled black hair tumbled unsheared and curly across the pale width of forehead disclosed by his shoved-back Stetson. Wind and glare had given his face the darkburnt look of carved mahogany, but it was the eyes which told Price's story.

* * *

At Safford he saw the girl again and this time turned for a fuller view as she got out of the stage on the arm of a corpulent drummer. She must have felt Price's stare because she pulled up her head, meeting his look with a pair of thoroughly cool eyes, the color of new grass, which disconcertingly surprised him by smiling. With a word of thanks to the drummer she went off by herself, obviously out to stretch her legs and see what sights the stop gave time for.

Price leaned against the shove of the wind in the grayness of dawn looking thoughtfully after her and wondering about her. She was young and full-bodied and astonishingly self-

4

possessed considering the shabby drabness of the clothes she'd chosen to travel in. Probably some out-at-elbows homesteader's daughter or perhaps a new schoolmistress enroute to the backlands.

When Hi Henry called 'Leavin'!' and climbed to his perch above the rumps of the horses Price, helping the girl aboard, climbed in after her, sliding into the last empty seat and leaving the spluttering drummer to the whip of the wind and the driver's tall yarning.

Of the five persons sharing the coach with himself, Price judged the whiskered individual seated on his right to be a small-spread cowman, the fellow on his left to be a San Carlos Apache and the two fellows flanking the girl just across from him to be cowhands of about the same age as himself. These last appeared very much smitten with the girl and the taller of the pair, in an apparent endeavor to impress her, was giving his talking talents full rein.

She smiled politely from time to time as the man enlarged upon the various abilities which had made him indispensable to the outfit currently employing him. She offered no comment of her own and at last, having run out of any further things to brag on, the fellow said, 'What about you? New to these parts, ain't you?'

'I don't suppose I'm what you'd call an "old settler."'

'Don't reckon you're more'n nineteen, are you?'

'You didn't tell me you were a judge of ladies ages.'

The tall puncher passed the palm of a hand across his mustache. 'I can generally pick 'em,' he conceded complacently. 'You wouldn't be related to Jid Tolliver, would you?'

'I'm afraid not,' she said. 'Do I resemble Mr. Tolliver?'

He inspected her reflectively. 'Your hair's about his color—got considerable more shine to it though than Jid's has. You ain't a schoolma'arm, are you?'

'Is there a vacancy around here?'

'Someone was saying they need a teacher for the Haines Holler schoolhouse,' the whiskered rancher put in, and the girl told him, smiling, that she was afraid she couldn't help them, not having any certificate.

'They wouldn't make no fuss about that,' Whiskers told her.

'Where you gettin' off at?' the tall puncher asked, smoothing his soup-strainer again.

'Which place would you suggest?'

He looked at her a moment as though half suspecting her of trying to pull his leg. 'I'm gettin' off at Geronimo myself. That's a good lively town—'

'Reckon it was lively enough when they hung that rustler,' Whiskers put in dryly. 'Is it true, what they claim, that his head was—'

6

The rest was lost in a squeal of brake blocks as the driver pulled up before a tin-roofed store in a cloud of gray-brown dust. 'Pima!' With a protesting shriek of leather the inside of the coach rocked sickeningly forward and then shuddered sideways as Hi Henry, trailed by the weight of the still grumbling drummer, came down over the wheel. 'Ten minutes!' he called, and tramped into the store with a mail bag.

'I think,' the girl said with green glance meeting Price's, 'I would like to get out and catch a breath of fresh air.'

Price, shoving open the door, stepped down and helped her out, ignoring the glare of the tall mustached hombre who appeared to have imagined she'd been speaking to him. The obese and derby-hatted drummer, having secured his case of samples from the racked luggage on the roof, was waddling after Hi Henry into the store.

The whiskered rancher thrust his head out and, hauling the rest of him after it, got down cuffing billows of dust from coat and trousers. He grinned through this haze and touched his hat to the girl. 'Sure hope you get where you're bound for in good shape, ma'am. Should you happen to decide to look into that Haines Holler job you tell 'em Doug Helper said you're just what they're huntin' for.'

'I'll remember,' she smiled back at him—'and thanks.'

7

A mounted cowpuncher, very freckled, edged out of the shadows of a nearby cottonwood with the reins on a lead pony clamped in gloved hand and the rancher, saying, 'Good luck, ma'am,' climbed into the saddle.

'That mustached whippoorwill bothering you?' Price asked as, with her hand on his arm, he toured her into the cool shadows beneath the green and yellow leaves.

She glanced from the sides of her eyes at him, softly laughing as though at an unexpected bit of banter. 'You don't believe I am able to look out for myself?'

There was an allusive fragrance about her like the smell of clean pine and, beneath her tiny hat, she had the reddest kind of hair he had ever got a look at. Her voice was husky; sort of deep, he thought, enormously attractive.

He told her somewhat stiffly, 'A young girl traveling solo—'

'I'm older than I look—I'm twenty-two,' she said impulsively. 'And, besides, I'm not.'

'Not what?'

'Traveling alone.'

Price looked down at her hands. They were ungloved, exquisitely smooth, long fingered and very shapely. He saw no rings but said, with the hint of a frown, 'You're with that drummer?'

The green eyes laughed up at him. 'Of

course I am—and with you, too. And the Indian. Not to mention the animated beanpole supporting that straw-colored mustache. How could anyone be alone wedged into a space that isn't sufficient even to accommodate a full-grown sardine?'

Price laughed. He had never met anyone so completely natural. 'Be cooler when we get up off this desert. You going very far?'

'Quite a way,' she said, and they walked awhile in silence.

She wasn't really pretty, he decided. But she had an appeal which, combined with their nearness, was getting its hooks into hungers long buried, making him too conscious of their closeness.

He freed his arm and got out the makings, tapering a smoke up and licking the paper. Afterwards, when he had got the thing lighted, she put her arm back in his again, looking off toward the unshaded scatter of houses.

'Have you ever found yourself wondering what kind of people live in places like this?'

'Pretty much the same as you'll find anywhere, I reckon.'

She sighed. 'Do you really think so?'

'Human nature,' Price said, 'doesn't appear to take much notice of the climate or color of skin God's wrapped around it.'

The store door slammed. The driver came out, glanced around and called, 'Leavin'!'

Price, watching him masticate a fresh chunk

of twist, guided the girl toward the coach; and she said as they approached, 'You seem to know your way around here. Have you ever come across a man named Fenwick?—Bryce Fenwick, I think his name is.'

Price's jaws ground together. He took the next several steps with his glance straight ahead, steel-gray eyes about as chummy as a couple of whetstones.

The hand on his arm became embarrassingly intimate but when, just short of the stage, he slanched a hard look at her, he found her peering up at him in the silence of pure astonishment.

'I guess you have,' she said; and Price, rather bleakly, nodded. 'I guess,' she said, 'you're not very fond of him.'

'You can rake in the pot with that one.' He maneuvered her toward the door of the coach.

She seemed to try to hold back, her fingers tightening their grip. Her green glance searched his face. 'You don't have to bundle me off like a leper. My name is Joyce Darling. I'm no relation to him.'

'Does it matter?' Price asked and, mounting the wheel, let his weight settle onto the box beside Henry. The driver gave him a fishy stare, waited long enough for the girl to climb inside, then eased off his brake and cracked his whip over the heads of the leaders.

*   *   *

They rolled a good piece with no talk between them, Henry attending to what he was hired for and Price taken up with a run of dark fancies called up by the name of the man who ran Turkey Track.

The day crawled along. The country got rougher with the mesquite and greasewood of the flats giving way to wolf's candle, pear and an occasional saguaro.

After awhile Price became uncomfortably aware of Hi Henry's covert regard. He ignored this as long as he could and then said irritably, 'Well, what's eating on you?'

The driver chewed for a spell in morose silence, then he spat out his cud, slashed an oblique look at the crusty expression on his passenger's face and declared in a tone of mortal injury, 'I like a man's kind of man,' and clamped his mouth shut again.

Price, after chucking a curious look at him, presently asked, 'And what kind is that?'

'Wal, it shore ain't the kind I got sidin' me this mornin'.'

Price looked himself over. 'I don't get it,' he said.

'I like a sociable man when I got to have somebody sharin' this box. Drivin' stage ain't no sinecure. When a feller's been doin' it fer forty year, day in an' day out in all kinds of weather, a-starin' at the hind ends of a bunch of misguided contrary critters like as genially

11

gits loaded into this yere harness, he's apt to git to honin' fer the sound of a human voice.'

'What do you want me to do,' Price said— 'sing!'

Henry gave him an edgy glance and growled: 'No! Last cowprodder that tried that aboard of me came within a inch of gettin' us turned over. It was on that bend twistin' down into Globe—feller sounded like a she-coyote about to give up the death rattle. Durn team went wilder'n a bunch o' March hares—never got 'em stopped till we was dang nigh t' Claypool! So, if it's all the same to you, I'd just rather hear you talk.'

'Any special topic you'd like to have exercised?'

Hi Henry peered around and then he sat awhile considering. He finally reached a hand behind him and wrenched his twist from a stuffed hip pocket. With jaw well stoked he spat and said, 'That strawberry roan say her last name was Darlin'?'

Through a considerable spell of hoof plop and harness shriek Price's stare rummaged the amber streaked growth of silvery bristles behind which the driver's red face was ambuscaded. 'Ain't it?'

The old man said aggrievedly, 'How in Tophet would *I* know?'

'It didn't sound like you were asking just to hear your teeth clack.'

'There you go gettin' riled again! Relax an'

12

git some good from your breathin'. She's been through here before. I can't recollect when nor the wherefors of it, but a man don't fergit a head o' hair like that. An' her bringin' up Fenwick! It's sure bustin' me what connection a high-steppin' filly like her could have with that skunk.'

It had been exercising Price too, though he didn't see fit to say so. 'She said she wasn't related to him.'

'I kin hear as good as the next man.'

'Well,' Price shrugged, 'it's no skin off my nose. She's free, white and twenty-two by her tell of it. I ain't been asked to pick her friends for her.'

The driver's shoe-button eyes flicked a look across Price as though his passenger were something he figured the cat had dragged in.

'I'd as lief turn her in with a corralful of wolves as to see her have truck with that stripe of polecat. I like a man's kind of man,' he said testily. 'If I was a young buck of your size an' build—'

'I've got plenty of fish of my own to set frying without borrowing trouble from any redheaded woman.'

CHAPTER TWO

Nevertheless, when Hi Henry pulled up awhile later in a tree-shaded hollow to give the team a rest before the long haul into Ft. Thomas, Price went down over the wheel with his mind more concerned with the girl than he'd have admitted. Although he could not put his finger on quite how she was able to manage it, there was something about this redheaded dish that sure as hell's hinges got a man plumb restless.

Price had no intention of hunting up a white charger or climbing into a pair of tin pants on her behalf, but he couldn't see the harm in granting himself another look at her.

Joyce Darling she'd said her name was, and he hadn't been able to shake the conviction this had meant something to the garrulous driver. Like Henry, Price wondered where she'd heard of Bryce Fenwick, who ranched a big jag of the hills beyond Sunflower and rather fancied himself a kind of bull of the woods.

Sloan hadn't yet put any location to Price's employment but, if the job was to take him within proximity of Fenwick, he'd be worse than a fool were he to pass up any chance which might tend to give him even the ghost of an advantage.

With some halfbaked notion rattling around

through his thinking he came up beside the coach in what had all the earmarks of being an uncommonly heavy silence. While he stood there hesitant, wondering if perhaps he mightn't better stroll elsewhere, the thorough-braces skreaked as under the weight of a shifted body and the girl's voice said abruptly: 'Didn't your mother ever tell you not to fool with strange young women?'

The coach door yawned open and the high rear end of the mustached masher from Geronimo backed precipitately out of the vehicle's explosive depths to fetch him, ears flaming, so near Price's arms could have completely encircled him.

'Need any help?'

The fellow's head slewed around as though a heel fly had bitten him.

'Pretty warm in there, I reckon,' Price surmised; and the man, looking minded to take a swipe at him, shoved him out of the way and, with an expression strangely scrambled, clambered up to perch beside the hairy-cheeked Henry.

Price winked at the latter. 'That your man's kind of man? Pretty rugged specimen to be getting coach sick, ain't he?'

The man's face turned red again but when he didn't seem disposed to make anything of it Price climbed inside and the horses lunged into their collars.

Although Price hadn't seen the Indian get off, the seat which he'd been warming was now completely unoccupied and the only person jouncing on the one beside the girl was the short and chunky puncher the mustached one had called 'Gobbler.' He was not doing any gobbling that Price was able to notice but was confining his attention to the vista reeling past the dusty frame of the nearest window. And the girl, over on her side, was looking out of hers.

Price, disposing himself with what comfort he could on the vacated leather across from them, spent the next several miles covertly admiring Joyce's profile.

They lunched at Ft. Thomas where the chunky puncher left them, and stopped for fresh horses at Bylas. They had a supper, of sorts, at another horse change high in the mountains surrounded by the splendor of red-barked pines, The sun disappeared in a red haze of glory which the girl watched breathlessly.

It was getting dark fast when they got under way again and a considerable drop in temperature moved Miss Darling to ask if he could not close some of the windows.

While he was unstrapping the leather curtains and snapping them into place Price inquired if she'd prefer to have him ride with

16

the driver.

'Do I make you uncomfortable?'

Price colored a bit and said gruffly that he thought she might like to catch a few winks of shut eye.

'Oh, I'm not the least sleepy. All my life I've wanted to come to Arizona and, now that I'm here, I simply can't see enough of it. Do you think there'll be a moon?'

'I shouldn't wonder.'

'What town are we going to come to next?'

'Sunflower,' Price said, with his thoughts wandering off to the prospective meeting with Sloan.

'Is it a very large place?'

'It'll be a rough one tonight if the crews from the ranches happen to be in with their pay checks. I'd advise you to keep these curtains pulled.'

She said with gentle raillery, 'You don't imagine anyone would attempt to bother me, do you?'

He could not in this gloom make out her expression but, gauging her mood correctly, he said, 'You can't tell what a man'll do when he's been soaking up whisky,' and made up his mind that, when they rolled to a stop before the Orrison Hotel, he'd stick right where he was until he heard Hi Henry yell 'Leavin'!' She was just young enough, and just brash enough it seemed like, to launch quite a commotion if there were no one around to keep a hand on

17

the reins.

He wondered if she knew the way her brand of looks could affect a man; and then the stage was tipping forward and the wind was a waterfall sound whipping round it and he heard the grind of brake blocks endeavoring to offset the rush of increased momentum; and, by these things, he knew they were running Old Baldy's flank on the final lap of their drop into town.

The girl through the gloom leaned abruptly toward him.

'Tell me one thing,' she said and Price, bracing himself for a repetition of the question she'd put to him earlier, nodded. 'I'd like to know,' she told him, 'how much Jonathan Crispin's word is worth in this country.'

'You mean Crispin, the land agent?' Price asked, surprised.

'The one who has offices in Phoenix?'

Price frowned, considering. 'It's a little hard to know what's the fair thing to tell you. In matters of appraisal he has a good rep for competence. But I think if the fellow were out to unload something it might pay a person to keep a sharp eye on him.' He wished he could make out her face a little plainer. 'You're not figuring to buy any land around here, are you?'

He reckoned that was ridiculous even as he asked it. She didn't look as if she could afford to buy enough ground to sit on.

He thought she smiled a bit herself. She said

with the careless lift of a hand, 'It was just something I've been wondering about. What you might, if you were a lawyer, call a "hypothetical" question.'

One thing Price was sure of. This redheaded piece might well be a schoolmarm but she didn't have the cut of any homesteader's daughter. Those carefully mended and madeover clothes could be the signs of somebody's plunge to poverty, but her choice of words bespoke an education far beyond the means of any plow-binding weedbender.

Never in his life had he met anyone so bewildering—such a delectable bundle of contradictions.

And then the stage was pulling up before the gray unpainted sheeting of the Orrison Hotel. 'Sunflower!' Henry shouted, and they could hear him pawing round among the baggage on the roof. Probably getting down Price's warsack.

The girl was unfastening a curtain. 'I'll be all right,' she said. 'Go ahead and wet your whistle if that's what you've had your mind on. There's a bar in the hotel, isn't there?'

She had the leather back now. A damp wind flowed in, blowing cold off the mountain. Price could hear the night sounds of this town turning up and he could see the girl's face, brightly etched against shadows.

'Reckon I'll wait here.'

'That's entirely unnecessary.'

19

'Reckon I'll wait anyhow.'

Her green eyes looked amused; and then some thought chased the raillery out of them and they were like two round rocks, hard and adamant as jade. 'Either you're getting out of this vehicle or I shall. I'll not have any man playing wet nurse to me.'

'If that's the way you want it,' Price said, straightening, 'I'll oblige you.'

His expression was still riled when he crossed the dingy lobby and, tossing his warsack into a corner, made for the bar. Maybe he could use that drink after all, he thought angrily. He certainly needed something before he went up to that talk with Sloan.

He dropped a cartwheel on the scrubbed pine and told the apron to fetch him two fingers of the best and a glass of icewater to cut the grime from his system.

He drank the icewater first and had just got around to hoisting the Old Crow when he realized how quiet the place had got in the last few seconds.

Instantly alert he slanted a glance at the back bar mirror, uncovering a line of frozen faces. Still holding the shot glass Price turned carefully around and then he saw where the trouble was coming from. Two guys at the back of the room were standing like a couple of dogs with their hackles up. The nearer, a gaunt spare shape in the clothes of a gambler, had his back turned to Price but there was no doubting the rage on the other man's face.

He was young, about Price's age, and garbed like a cowman and if his face hadn't been so hardtwisted with anger it would probably have been handsome.

Men were edging away from them when the gambler said something Price couldn't quite catch. With all the brashness of hell in his voice the cowman bawled, 'And I'll not tell you again to keep your stuff out of Bunchgrass! You keep on like you're doin, Flack, and one of these days they'll be findin' you buried there!'

'You want to settle this now?' Flack asked quietly.

The cowman's face turned red and then, furiously, white again.

'That would suit you fine, wouldn't it! Never fret, I'll settle it; but the time and the place will be my choosin'—and it won't be where any bunch of your trigger sharks'll be handy to blast me loose of my britches!'

Flack walked around the man. 'Doubt they'd fit me anyway,' he said, lifting a grin with a wink for the crowd. 'Why don't you go and cool off, Archer? You ought to know my crew can't watch those cows every minute. If you figure you've got a legitimate gripe, come along to the office and I'll send for Bryce—'

'And shoot the same old runaround. No thanks,' Archer sneered. 'I can take care of

21

mine without no fofaraw from Fenwick.'

'Suit yourself. But just remember Bunchgrass Basin is a three-way split—'

'If that bunch you got on South Ranch would remember that—Ahr,' Archer said explosively. 'What the hell good are words? You don't catch none of my stock gettin' into that grass! The deal you an' Turkey Track made with my Dad—'

Flack said impatiently, 'I know what the deal was. The trouble's with the cattle. All grass looks alike to them—'

'Words!' Archer spat and, shoving men off his elbows, plowed a track toward the batwings. But as he started to push through, the rage inside him twisted his head around. 'If I see any more of your cattle trampin' that grass they're goin' to damn sure be dead ones. And the same thing goes for Fenwick's—you can tell him that from me!'

*   *   *

The quiet didn't leave with Archer; it hung on until the gambler, with a wry little smile toward a wedge-shaped face beneath a black Texas hat, passed around the bar's elbow and slid through a door marked OFFICE, carefully shutting it behind him.

All the room's normal sounds began to drum up then behind the buzz of conversations and Price, still without sampling his whisky,

22

returned his belly to the pine, inscrutably following the Texan in the mirror. The man was thinner than Flack, built like a snake on stilts, with a pair of unwinking cat-yellow eyes in his head and a bone-handled pistol packed butt forward in a leather thonged rigid against his right leg.

Price watched till the fellow shoved through to the street and then considered his whisky with a faraway frown.

He had heard a thing or two about that basin deal when he'd been up here before to get those heifers from Fenwick. Archer's old man, after they'd run off the soddy trying to farm the place, had entered into an agreement with Anvil and Turkey Track to rest up the land and get some feed back onto it.

That had been some while back and the understanding was that, when they'd got the browse built up enough, the parties to the deal would take it turn and turn about, each to have the use of it every third season. The seeds of discord had been sown when Flack, who was a power in town, had bought out Anvil's owner and forthwith let it be known he aimed to have first crack at that grass when it was used again.

Archer's old man, who'd been on the timid side, hadn't put up any argument. But a horse had piled him up last year when Price, on behalf of Pumpkin, had been here dickering with Fenwick; and it looked like the son might hold a different view of matters.

Not that Price gave a rip one way or the other. If Archer, Flack and Fenwick wanted to shoot each other up he certainly wasn't figuring to grab a hold on anyone's shirttail. Be a darn good thing for this country if they *all* wound up on a shutter.

Still his mind kept turning it over, considering and reconsidering how such a situation might affect the deal he had made with Sloan. It didn't seem too likely that his job with Soan could have anything to do with this locality. He'd never heard tell of any Sloans in these parts nor heard of any spread that could be bought around Sunflower.

He reckoned he'd better wash up and go see the old coot.

Tossing off his drink and picking up his change he went back to the lobby and, shouldering his warsack, moved over to the counter and asked for a room. He didn't ask if Sloan were registered here; he took a look for himself while he was signing his name.

He didn't have to look far. *E. D. Sloan, El Paso, Texas,* was boldly inscribed upon the line above his own. 'Not superstitious, are you?' the clerk asked with a grin. The disc on the key he shoved toward Price was stamped 13. Sloan had drawn Room 10.

Price shrugged and, on some inexplicable prompting, stepped over to the window and had a look at the street. The stage had gone. He heaved a kind of sigh, thinking briefly of

24

Miss Darling. Then he tramped up the stairs, located the door that matched his key, went in and, shoving it shut, dropped his warsack on the bed.

If the old man had waited this long, Price reckoned it wouldn't hurt him none to continue twiddling his thumbs a few minutes longer.

Getting out of his shirt, he scrubbed himself and got a fresh shield-fronted one out of his duffle. He wiped the dust from his boots with the one he'd taken off, ran a hand through his rebellious hair and finally blew out the light.

He didn't know why he should feel nervous about this meeting, nor why he should think of Sloan as old except that ranchers mostly were by the time they'd salted away enough cash to indulge in the luxury of hiring themselves managers. He reminded himself to be properly respectful, thinking that any fellow who could pay the wage E. D had promised had a lot of it coming—or should have his head examined.

He rapped on Number 10 and heard a muffled voice call: 'Just a minute,' and was wondering if maybe he should have strapped on his gun when metal clacked in metal and the door was pulled open.

It would have been hard to say which was the more astounded, but the bottom of Price's jaw pretty nearly hit the floor when he recognized Joyce Darling.

The lamp was somewhere back of her,

leaving her face in shadow, but no one else had hair like that; and he was backing away when she said indignantly, 'We'd better get this straight. If you're presuming to imagine you can trade—'

'Now just a minute. I didn't follow you up here; didn't even know you'd stayed in this town.'

'Then what was the idea pounding on my door?'

'I didn't know it was your door. Gosh almighty! I came up here looking for—'

Price abruptly stopped with his mouth still open, taking in the belted Levis and the man's blue woollen shirt she wore. He was still like that, still staring, when she asked, 'Is your name *Price*?'

He could only nod.

She suddenly laughed and stepped back. 'Then you're looking for Sloan. I guess you'd better come in.'

CHAPTER THREE

Inside, when the door shut, Price came about with a crusty stare. 'Where you keeping him—in that tobacco tin?'

'You're looking right at him.'

'Maybe I better get out my spectacles.'

'*I'm* Sloan,' she said, smiling.

'I guess I ain't been hearing good, either. I seem to've got the idea your name was Joyce Darling.'

She uncovered the shine of her milk white teeth. 'Of course it is. But it can also be Sloan—'

'When you're fixing to fool someone.'

Her expression became bitter. 'How many answers do you think I'd have got if that ad had appeared in the name of a woman?'

'What else you got up your sleeve you ain't told yet?'

'Look,' she said, tight of cheek, 'if you don't want this job you can say so right now!'

Price's jaw ridged with muscle. The girl's green eyes never wavered. Price said finally, grudgingly, 'No man likes to figure he's been played for a sucker.'

'You weren't.'

'You ain't paying all that money for any knowhow with cattle!'

'Do I look like a fool? I told you fair and square in that ad what I wanted—a man who can't be bluffed or backed down.'

'I'm no gun man,' Price growled.

'I could get any number of gun-hung drifters for what I offered you. I want a man I can depend on—'

'You can't buy loyalty with dollars and cents.'

'No law against my trying. If you don't like the idea, now is the time to say so.'

27

Some color got into Price's cheeks and he said angrily, 'I took this job with my eyes open. Let's quit sparring around and get down to brass tacks. You've got a ranch, I suppose?'

'I've got the land on which to build one.'

Price glared at her. 'Where is it?'

'According to Jonathan Crispin it's about a two hours ride from here—'

'You bought this place from Crispin?'

'I bought it from the state for back taxes.'

Price took a caged turn around the room. When he could trust himself to speak he said, 'This state gives the owner five years to reclaim it. Have you considered your position if, after having built this place up, the real owner comes along and decides to take over?'

She said coolly, 'Certainly. He'll have to make good the money I've paid out in taxes and pay for every dollar of improvements I've put into it.' She pushed back her hair, smiling thinly. 'He's the one part of this deal you'll not have to do any worrying about.'

Price, groaning under his breath, said, 'This property got any handle to it?'

'I believe it's known pretty generally as Bunchgrass Basin.'

*   *   *

Price stared for nearly five seconds hand-running before her face swung into clear focus. He presently dug the makings from a pocket

28

and, as mechanically, thrust them away unopened.

'I suppose you know what you're doing,' he said.

'Of course I know what I'm doing.'

'That makes everything just lovely.' He drew a ragged breath. 'What do you propose doing about Flack, Archer and Fenwick?'

She considered him with a climbing eyebrow. 'What about them.'

'They've been tangling over that place already.'

'I believe Crispin did say something along those lines. I understood him to say they'd been "resting" the land. He said there had been practically no cattle on that ground in eight years.'

'It's a pretty safe bet there'll be some on it shortly.'

'That's true. I've a thousand head on the way right now. From Texas. They should be eating that grass inside of another week—'

'You don't suppose those outfits will let 'em, do you?'

'If you mean Anvil, Spanish 40 and Turkey Track—'

'That's exactly who I mean. Flack, Archer and Fenwick.'

'They've no legal standing in the Basin at all. They can't even show the right of use. I've looked into that end of it thoroughly—'

'You ever looked into the business end of a

six-shooter?'

Her left eyebrow followed the right one up this time and she stood there a moment staring loftily at him. Then, raising her arms in a languorous yawn, she ran long fingered hands through that mop of red hair, trapping his glance with the way her young breasts thrust against the tight front of that snug-fitting shirt.

'Are you endeavoring to frighten me?'

Price felt like hitting her.

He said disgustedly, 'You think, just because you've got a hideful of curves, those boys are going to set back and let you get away with it? You go in there with them cattle and you're going to have trouble.'

'You expected to *earn* that hundred and fifty, didn't you?'

'I'm no miracle man!'

'Then you'd better brush off whatever talents you've got because I'm paying for the best and I shall certainly expect to get it. We'll need horses,' she said over her shoulder, crossing the room. She pulled a roll of bills from a drawer and tossed five twenties on the burn-scarred top of a table. 'Have two saddled and ready and wake me up at three o'clock.'

'By God, you've got your nerve—I'll say that for you.'

The green eyes rummaged his face with a smile. 'Do you know anything a faint heart ever won?'

Price, involuntarily, was drawn a step closer.

But she waved him away with a throaty chuckle. 'Run along now, Morgan. And don't forget we ride at three.'

*   *   *

In his mind, as Price went down the stairs, were a good many thoughts, and not a one of them comfortable. And the more he considered them the blacker his mood got. Everything he'd learned, every move he saw ahead, seemed designed to plunge this range into the bitter animosities of a full-scale fight for grass.

He did not require any crystal ball to foresee how the squabbling combine would take this. They'd already run one fellow out to get hold of it and, after resting the place all this while for their own stock, they were not going to fool around chewing their cuds while any chit of a girl from outside breezed in and reaped the benefit of what they had schemed for.

There was only one place in town where he could hire or buy horses at this time of the night, the Copper State Feed & Livery, and in the knowledge of the invasion this girl was proposing he thought a couple of times of going back for his pistol. It was the memory of Fenwick which made him discard the impulse.

He found the proprietor on a box outside the door enjoying the night's coolness. 'I'd like

31

a couple of sure-footed horses,' Price told him, 'and if you've got what I want I'll pay cash and take 'em outright.'

The old man fetched a lantern and they looked over what he had. Price chose a rangy streak-faced sorrel and a long-barreled short backed buckskin and got the pair for eighty dollars, with saddles and gear thrown in for thirty more. Since he'd already dug into his own cash for ten of it, he dug a little deeper and acquired a pair of rifles which the old man loaded for free.

'Throw a feed of grain in them around two o'clock,' Price told him, and went back to the Orrison.

At three o'clock he scratched on the girl's door. 'All right, Sloan, climb out of it,' he grunted. 'I've got the horses waiting and a cold snack tucked away on the saddles.'

She joined him ten minutes later at the bottom of the stairs. She was dressed much the same as she'd been last night in shirt and Levis. To these she had added a pair of spurred boots and there was a cream-colored hat pinned on top of her hair. 'You've fetched something to drink, haven't you?'

'Canteen of java and a canteen of water—you want a jug of wine, too?'

In the lonesome light of a low-turned bracket he caught a flash of white teeth as she looked round with a smile.

'Do you think you can find the place?' he

32

asked.

'I don't imagine I shall have any trouble about that.'

She swung into the saddle without accepting his help. They rode northwest out of town on the stage road to Globe.

'I had an idea,' Price said, reining abreast of her, 'that we'd be heading more south.'

'It's a little shorter that way. But there's a chain of low peaks we'd have to cross if we did and the Notch—the most accessible pass—climbs off of range claimed by Anvil. We're going in by Rugged Mesa; there's a trail of sorts cutting south just north of Parker's Peak. We're not so likely to be spotted going this way.'

'You're not going to get no thousand head of cattle in without having them spotted.'

'At least there's no use in worrying about that until they get here.'

'What are you calling this spread?' Price asked presently.

'The registered brand is Bar O.'

'Squabble O would sound a lot more like it,' Price said dryly. 'How much of this land have you paid taxes on?'

'The whole twelve thousand acres of it.'

'And you're expecting to build up a paying operation on a place of that size? Most of the cowmen I've known wouldn't consider that big enough to use for a horse trap—'

'I'm not like most of the cowmen you've

known.'

Price nodded soberly. 'You sure as hell ain't.'

It was too dark to make out her face in this murk but he had the sour conviction she was on the verge of laughing—her and Marie Antoinette, he thought glumly; and reckoned he had been forty kinds of a fool to throw up his job with Pumpkin for this kind of antic. Manager of a spread that probably wouldn't last the month out! But he was stuck with it now no matter how brash its concept; tied hand and foot by that hundred and fifty, which, by the way this deal looked about to shape up, he'd likely never touch a cent of.

As though divining his notions the girl swung round in her saddle. 'I'm not as crazy as you think. You've got it in your head these men intended using the basin as winter range, and I expect you're right. But you're taking a pretty dim view of things, Morgan. I'm not planning to ranch on any basis you're used to.

'You'll find I'm essentially a practical person. I didn't drive into this thing on an impulse. Bunchgrass Basin is blessed with plenty of water. It's got a stream running through it, springs and two or three lakes. It's well sheltered—rimmed north and east by mountains. The Red Hills and Rugged Mesa cut the winds from the west. A high ridge and The Roughs protect the southern flank of it. A proper pattern of fencing could make this

34

place a year-round range if the management had the wit to work with registered cattle.'

For a man used to free grass and stock grown mostly to bone and horn this was a pretty revolutionary thing she was saying. It took Price a while to get used to it. 'You mean—'

She did laugh now, a low intoxicating sound, as she said, 'Of course. That herd I'm bringing in is composed entirely of whitefaces. Registered Herefords—just think of it, Morgan!'

Price was trying to. He was making tough work of it. The gamble of the thing was shouldering out too many details; yet he couldn't help feeling excited. He had thought of her as brash but he knew now she was smart, too—she was miles ahead of these cowmen around here. He was enough of one himself to know that twelve thousand acres put to registered stock could do it, could pile up a fortune where the average spread would go broke.

Little by little he felt himself warming up to it. When he realized how enthusiastic he was becoming he hauled himself up with the other side of the picture. The side cast in shadow by the glowering faces of Flack, Archer and Fenwick. She'd found gold in these hills but would those wolves let her mine it?

Not, he thought grimly, if they were able to help it.

He said after awhile, 'Time will tell, I reckon. You got a spot picked out where we can throw up the buildings?'

'There are buildings on it. A small but comfortable ranch house. A bunkhouse. A blacksmith shop and harness shed. A big rambling barn that we can turn into stables.' There was eagerness in her voice, the kind of fondness of one who describes loved things remembered. 'Just wait until you see it— they're along the biggest lake in the shade of a grove of willows, and there's one great tall old cottonwood. Three men couldn't hardly get their arms around its trunk. Well have to build corrals, of course, and we may have to do some repairing on the roofs but everything we'll need's right there. Except, of course, the fences. The boys are bringing in the wire and posts for those with the herd.'

Price said, 'I can't make you out,' and watched her chin slowly lift through the darkness.

'Would it help if I carried a lantern?'

'Might at that,' he grunted.

'What particularly is itching you?'

He rode the creaking leather for several horse lengths, saying nothing. But all that he was thinking got its hooks in the voice with which he finally said, dissatisfied, 'You know too much, Sloan.'

'If you'd looked at those pictures, studied the map Crispin sent me—'

36

'Did he say what this bird had been trying to raise there?'

'Wheat, mostly. A little millo maize, I think, and perhaps a few apricots. Why?'

'Just wondering,' Price said absently. 'That Parker's Peak off there to the left?'

She looked and said she guessed so; she also said they'd have to stay with the stage road until they'd crossed the plank bridge above the gorge of Thief River. 'About a couple miles yet.'

Already some of the black was wearing out of the darkness. Price calculated the night ought to be pretty well departed by the time they came to the banks of the river. He wondered if Flack guessed what they were up to. The man was bound to be keeping an eye out. If he were half as shrewd as he appeared to be they might very well find someone waiting at that bridge.

He started to build up a smoke, thought better of it and said, 'What made you ask if I knew Bryce Fenwick?'

'Curiosity, I suppose. I wrote the postmaster at Sunflower—using, of course, a made-up name—asking about conditions here. The man I heard from was Fenwick. He described things as being pretty rough in this region, saying it took, generally speaking, around fifty acres to support one cow and that, in any event, there was nothing for sale here.'

'How long ago was that?'

'About six months.'

'And where did you write from?'

She took the question offhandedly, replying without appearing to give it much notice. 'Abilene.'

A line of gray in the east was opening up behind Old Baldy and, beyond it, the Santa Teresas began to poke their shapes above the black horizon. Day was not far off. Not as far as the bridge, he reckoned.

He lifted the sixshooter from his holster and replaced its cartridges with fresh loads from his belt. Just in case, he told himself, the ammunition had been tampered with. Ira Flack was no fool.

He could see the girl's face plainer now, enough to know the move had not gone unnoticed.

'Getting ready to earn that hundred and fifty?'

'I'll do what I have to.'

'I don't imagine we'll need to expect trouble yet. The word could hardly have—'

'The word,' Price said bluntly, 'went out when we got off that stage.'

She considered that, discarding it. 'I think you're jumping at shadows.'

'I'd a heap rather jump than have a hole shoveled over me.'

She grinned and Price said roughly: 'You're not playing for marbles! When you rile a bunch like this one—'

'I haven't riled them yet.'

'You've prodded them. You put them on guard when you wrote that letter.'

'They can't prove I wrote it.'

'They don't have to. These fellows didn't get where they're at in this country by shining the backs of their pants on a porch rail. In this kind of place—'

'And just what kind of place is it?'

'The kind you can expect where the marshal's the brother of the town's kingpin gambler. Every stranger, every saddle bum that's hit this region since you wrote that fool letter will have been gone over with a fine-tooth comb—and they won't overlook us.'

In the increasing brightness of the coming day he could see that she had gone very straight in the saddle. There was a soberness about her mobile mouth that looked unbending and the green eyes held the bleakness he had caught in them before. It was like seeing a different woman.

Then her eyes came around and met his and were amused again. 'And if you're right what do you think they'll be apt to do about it?'

'It won't be nothing to laugh about. You can damned well bet on that,' Price said.

'They'd hardly look for us to get up in the middle of the night.'

That old fellow at the livery would expect it, though, Price told himself. And he might not be above passing the word on.

'I think,' he said finally, 'they may have someone at the bridge. Whether they do or not, it's a cinch they'll have somebody watching the Basin.'

The girl didn't answer but reined her horse ahead impatiently.

When he got abreast again Price asked if she'd had the sale recorded.

'Naturally.'

'Where?'

'At the county seat, of course. I had it taken care of by mail when I paid the taxes.'

Dawn was brushing the eastern heavens a cherry red when they came onto a rise and saw the narrow bridge before them. The surroundings offered scant chance for an ambush and the only thing they saw as they crossed the rattling planks was the river, deeply blue, a hundred and forty feet below them.

Almost at once Joyce, taking the lead, swung south on what looked to have been in the remote past a wagon road. Thickly grown to weeds and crab grass, Price discovered no sign it had been used in quite some while.

The ground dropped rapidly downward through a tangle of ash and sycamore, a variety of birds chirping and scolding from their branches. Where the ground leveled off to a curl around a great mesa the river came out of its gorge with gay chucklings and a whitetail deer bounded away through the brush.

Another ten minutes of travel fetched them onto a bench and they had their first look at the platter-shaped valley this girl had staked claim to. It must certainly have delighted any cowman's eye. Straight south to the powder-blue smudge of what appeared to be bluffs the rolling land presented an emerald sea of waving grass.

'Where are the buildings?' Price asked curiously, and was astonished by the cold and naked fury of her look

He said, dropping a hand toward his pistol, 'What's the matter?'

'They've burned them!' she cried bitterly.

CHAPTER FOUR

And that was when the rifle cracked.

It was a high-powered gun and fired from so far back of beyond it made hardly more sound than the ghost of a whisper, but the first screaming messenger sped from its barrel spattered the buckskin's hoofs with grit and Price didn't wait for a second invitation.

He got off that horse like hell wouldn't have him. But he had presence of mind enough to drag his Winchester. Yelling for Joyce to get back into the brush he rolled for the cover of a potato-shaped boulder, closely pursued by two other scorched pellets. Only then did he

41

bother to take stock of his surroundings.

Now that he had a little time to think about it this bench didn't look much like a true job of nature. It was a fill which had been dumped into a fault of the canyon, diverting the river from its natural course. Beyond this boulder where he crouched he could see the old streambed curling off through the hollow left between bench and mesa.

Rock dust flew as lead ricocheted off the top of Price's boulder. But he'd been watching for it this time and spotted the faint haze of powder-smoke. The guy was up on the rim of that mesa, bedded down in a fringe of catclaw and juniper.

Price held his fire, remembering in time that he had scant ammunition to be wasting in such fashion. This was one of the pair of saddle guns he had got from that old man at the livery and while, conceivably, it would work it was no match for the artillery that bushwhacker was using. If its slugs would carry that far they would be too spent to constitute a threat, and only a threat of the very first order seemed likely to flush that fellow from his advantage.

Price debated the wisdom of dashing for his horse. He carefully twisted his neck around but could not pick up the buckskin's position. 'Hey, Sloan!' he called guardedly. 'You know where my horse went?'

'I've got him down here,' Joyce answered from the riverward side of the embankment.

'I'm coming after him,' Price said and, scrambling onto his haunches, made a headlong dive across the bench doubled over. It took the bushwhacker by surprise; yet, at that, he barely made it. One slug slammed Price's hat down across his left eye, another took off a bootheel.

'That sonofagun can shoot,' he growled, limping down through the brush to where the girl held the horses.

'You were right,' she said. 'They've had somebody watching this place.'

'All night,' Price grunted; and she asked him what he was going to do.

'Going after him, of course.'

'Do you think that's wise?'

'You want to spend the rest of your life here?'

'I don't imagine he'll wait that long—'

'I ain't waiting to find out.' Price inspected the Winchester to make sure it was loaded, then got into the saddle. 'You stick right here till I get that fellow's number.'

He rode the buckskin downstream for about forty yards and then, slapping him with the rein ends, sent him scampering up the bank. The bushwhacker fired as he topped it but Price didn't hear any wail from the bullet. What he heard was shod hoof sound and, twisting his head, he saw the girl on the sorrel flash up out of the brush.

Cursing, Price put spurs to the buckskin.

43

They went hellity-larrup down the bench's far side and into the abandoned bed of the river. Behind him the girl was banging away with her rifle. Price couldn't tell if the man was firing or not. All his faculties were fixed on finding a way up the mesa which his horse could negotiate. He rode a dodging and twisty hundred yards before he found what he was looking for, and when he got to the table-flat surface of the hill the man he was after was building a dust cloud halfway across it, trying to reach the far side.

Joyce set her horse up with front legs flying. 'Let him go,' she cried, and Price scowled at her irritably.

'You want him potting us tomorrow?'

'Please—' her eyes pleaded; and Price, without a word, turned his horse back down the trail.

When they got back onto the bench he said, 'You want to go on or have you got enough of it?'

'I'm going to town and hire some carpenters to come out here and throw up another set of buildings!'

She had spunk, all right.

But Price shook his head. 'You better think that over. In the first place I doubt if you could get any carpenters out here, and if you did—'

'I'll get them!'

'All right. How are you going to protect them? Smart thing to do is get a tent for the time being; when your crew gets in they can put up whatever's essential. And, speaking of crews, them fellows ought to be warned.'

He caught that hard amusement in her green eyes again. 'They're not expecting any picnic. You take care of the Combine and let me do the thinking—'

'I'm not the U.S. Cavalry, Sloan. I can't stand off that bunch if they come down on us in force—'

'They won't be expecting to need much force to discourage a pair of what they probably imagine to be squatters. If you can't handle a couple of irate ranchers.'

'Don't let that red hair get in the way of your judgment. I'll hold down the place. And while you're fetching your carpenters maybe you'd better take in my horse and fetch out a load of grub. Also some cartridges. And get this boot fixed.'

She took the boot. 'You'd better keep your mount. I'll hire a pack horse from the livery or a team and wagon if I can find one.'

She considered him a moment as though debating something further. But, whatever it was, she decided against it and, with a wave of her hand, rode off through the ash and sycamore, determinedly headed in the direction of the bridge.

*   *   *

45

Price, staring after her with mixed emotions, reckoned it might be the best thing for her if she did bump into trouble. Perhaps it would knock a little caution into her head; she sure could stand plenty of that, he thought sourly.

Hooking the knee of his bootless foot round the gleaming brass horn of his scuffed Hamely saddle, he considered disgustedly where this mess he'd tied into was taking him. It was not a long chore for, at the pace this headlong filly was taking them, there was only one conclusion he could logically accept. Something had to pop, and that was plain as plowed ground.

As the boss of her operations he could naturally expect to draw the most of the fire and, knowing something of the caliber of this bunch he'd have to deal with, he could see mighty easy it was going to be a hot one. He had no doubt at all but what he'd earn that hundred and fifty if he could avoid being planted before he even got started.

He frowningly shaped up a smoke as he went over things she had told him. Somewhere or other, it seemed, she'd got hold of Joe Crispin. Joe had fired up her fancy with a map and some pictures of this Bunchgrass Basin, probably telling her what could be done with the place if it was put to the raising of pedigreed cattle. Because the Combine had scared off the original owner and no one around here had sufficient guts to buck the big

46

outfits planning to use the place, she'd been able to pick up the Basin for taxes.

So much was clear. But it couldn't have looked the bargain you would naturally assume, because she'd admitted Crispin had told her what the Combine had been up to. She may quite possibly have imagined that, with the law on her side and being a woman, she could buck their game without any real violence.

Only Price couldn't swallow that. There was too much evidence to the contrary.

She was not as naive as she would have herself appear. She'd been weaned for quite some while, he reflected, recalling that hard look he'd caught about her eyes when things hadn't gone quite the way she'd figured they ought to. She had known this was going to make trouble or she wouldn't have advertised her need for a manager who couldn't be bluffed or backed down.

But, despite the irascible turn of Price's thinking, he could not help feeling a kind of grudging admiration for her temerity.

She was sharp as well as good-looking; a tough-minded woman who'd lined her sights on what she'd wanted and gone after it regardless. He guessed this wasn't any noticeably different than the notion which had got him into this himself. A desire to get ahead in the world was probably universal. He didn't think, just the same, it set too well on a woman.

Uncurling his leg from the horn he ground his cigarette out on his oxbow stirrup and sent the long-barreled buckskin toward the skyward thrust of a distant butte. Its rocky shape rose above the rippling green of the Basin about a third of the way between himself and the powder-blue smudge of the bluffs which the girl had said bounded the southern flank of her holdings.

Three-quarters of an hour of leisurely riding fetched the butte into fairly sharp focus. He could see the trees now beyond and to the left of it which marked the approximate site of the former ranch headquarters, those buildings the girl had so peculiarly described; and he wondered about that while the buckskin turned of its own accord and, with a quickening pace, ambled toward them.

'Smells the water,' Price thought; and then, with sudden sharp suspicion, looked the gelding over for brand marks. It packed the Terrapin iron on its off hip, and Price snorted. He reckoned his thinker must have run off its track; but just the same he stopped the horse and got down for a closer look at the mark. Limping back to the animal's head Price pinched back its lip and had a stare at its teeth, afterwards swearing.

Climbing back in the saddle he sent the buckskin quartering toward the shine of a yonder lake, pulling up in a burned-over area some twenty rods this side of it. He sat awhile, morosely regarding the charred and lifeless trunk of what had once been a gigantic cottonwood. There was nothing left of the former ranch structures. The iron rims and one hub of a vanished wagon lay off to the side, rust red and half buried in the untracked dirt.

But the fire which, devouring the buildings, had killed off that grandfather cottonwood was no fresh piece of villainy. It was something which had happened a good while ago, and proof of this was indisputably afforded in the limbs and green-yellow foliage of several twelve-foot-high thickets of broomweed growing out of the discolored earth.

So where had Crispin gotten the pictures?

Price rode back to the bench and, again climbing onto the mesa, poked around along the rim until he found where those slugs had been pumped from. This ground was well packed and there was nothing of an illuminating nature to be seen except the gleaming jackets of a number of spent cartridges.

He sat pondering these awhile, at last swinging down with a grunt to pick up one. The nooning shafts of the overhead sun struck up a golden glinting as he lazily chunked it around in his palm. Just about what he'd figured—a .45-90. But as he swept back his hand to pitch it away something caused him to pause and reconsider it. The shell was a rim fire product; but the thing which had caught at Price's notice was the letter, indented on the metal's firing surface. It was an initial he had never before encountered on a cartridge case and, getting back in the saddle, he tucked the tarnished bit of brass into his pants' watch pocket.

With a thoughtful frown he sent the buckskin across the mesa in the direction toward which the man who'd fired it had been heading. Superimposed against the bright glare coming off the baked expanse of unbroken flat ahead of him, he saw the girl's face as it had been when she had cried so imperiously, 'Let him go!' And he found something there to be concerned about also.

Every facet of this thing, as he got around to uncovering it, seemed to point inexorably to something else, still hidden.

At the mesa's far side he found where the bushwhacker had quit it. The rim was broken over here by several ancient slides and on the talus littered slope of one of these he saw the tracks the fellow's horse had made and followed them with narrowed eyes to the dust-dry surface of the alkali plain below. The man had struck off across this without pause, heading west with considerable speed past the yawning mouths of two south-angling canyons. Something about the look of that second one struck a responsive chord in Price's memory and, abruptly, he recalled the name of it. Shaketree Canyon!

He gave a short mirthless laugh.

Some three miles west and south of Shaketree's upper entrance were the headquarters buildings of Turkey Track. And it was in that canyon Fenwick had tried to shortcount him on those heifers he had bought for Two Pole Pumpkin. And there also, as he'd been about to pull out for the long drive home, Bryce Fenwick had furiously told him never to set foot in this country again.

CHAPTER FIVE

The sun was rolling low behind the purple outline of a distant saddle-shaped mountain when Price, from the shade of a couple stunted pinons growing out of the mesa's north rim, saw dust where the stage road from town climbed the approach to the rattling plank bridge spanning the gorge of Thief River.

As the crow flies that bridge was scarcely more than a mile from where Price, throughout the day, had been keeping his eye peeled; and he was presently able to see beneath the dust the laboring shapes of a team and wagon with a saddled horse hitched to its tail gate.

Two persons occupied the seat and the

shapes of a couple more could be seen bouncing around in the bed of the wagon among shifting mounds of groceries and implements. The driver was a man and it was Joyce who sat beside him—even from here Price could see the burnished luster of her hair.

He hoped she had had a good meal in town because he'd pretty well consumed all the grub he had packed on his saddle.

It had been a long wait, sitting around with nothing to do but think and stare. Price had chosen this spot for his vigil because it overlooked most of the approaches likely to be taken if the fellow who had shot at them decided to come back with help.

But Price had seen nothing more of him.

Several solitary riders had crossed the bridge bound for town but none of these had been Fenwick. Any one of them, however, might have been in Fenwick's pay; and it was Price's considered opinion that one of them probably had been dispatched with word of the intrusion to one or the other of Fenwick's associates—probably Flack.

Price couldn't think how the girl figured to get a wagon down that trail considering the shape it was in. But she had a knack for getting things done, it would seem, were one to judge by the fact that she had fetched three men with her where Price would have sworn she wouldn't even get a boy.

He threw the hull on the buckskin and picked up his rifle. Might as well get along down there, he guessed, and got into the saddle. As there was no way down from this point of the mesa, he jogged back across the barrens to the place he had come up at, sitting there awhile and turning over his thoughts. No hurry about getting down because, even if the crew with Joyce had axes and shovels, it would take them two or three hours to fetch that wagon to the bench.

When it began to get dark he put the horse down into the abandoned bed of the river, satisfied the bushwhacker would not be bothering them short of daylight.

He could hear the sound of horse hoofs and the skreak and jolt of a rumbling wagon as he came onto the bench and, guessing how keyed up those men with Joyce might be, he ground-hitched the buckskin and began scouting dead wood in the riverbank growth below the embankment.

He soon had a good-sized blaze on the bench. The Combine—Fenwick anyway—already knew of their presence, so the fire wasn't going to give anything away. Except their whereabouts; and that would have to be chanced in the interest of other things.

He was dropping another couple armfuls of wood on the pile when the girl rode up out of the shadows. 'Well,' he said, 'I see you made it all in one piece.'

'And I notice you're still above ground without patches.' She smiled. 'Here's your boot.'

Price pulled it on as she swung out of the saddle. 'You get the cartridges?'

'I didn't encounter any insurmountable difficulty locating carpenters once I let it be known I was prepared to pay top wages. I've hired six. The boss and two others are bringing up the wagon—I got plenty of groceries. The others are coming out with the lumber in the morning. Well—aren't you going to congratulate me?'

'I'll save the congratulations until the buildings are up.' He didn't tell her this was working out too easy but the thought was in his mind. 'Are those cartridges on the wagon?'

She seemed faintly embarrassed, and cold barbs of unease sank deep into Price's thinking when she said, 'They're out of those sizes but the storekeeper's expecting another shipment in next week—I'm sure he was telling the truth, Morg.'

'Did he take you back and show you?'

She said, 'As a matter of fact, he did,' and Price nodded. 'I got that tent, too,' she added. 'It will probably come in handy, and I can be using it while they're putting up the buildings.'

Price, turning away, swung back to say irritably, 'You're setting too much store by those buildings, Sloan.'

'Why?'

'Because, in this kind of deal, it's smart to take first things first. The first thing you've got to prove to this county is the ability to hang onto this place now that you've got it.'

'You worry too much,' she said, smiling. 'In a court fight the worth of improvements—'

'This won't come to no court. What law there is around here won't be used to your benefit. The marshal's Flack's brother and you're up against a bunch that's used to having their way—'

'You don't have to shout. I'm not hard of hearing.'

'Then don't be so damned stubborn! You haven't suckered anybody fetching out those carpenters; you wouldn't have got 'em if the Combine wasn't willing.'

She said with her chin up, 'The only point worth considering is that I've managed to get them; the whys need not concern us.'

Price gave her a jaundiced stare, abruptly shrugged and tramped off toward the river on the trail of more firewood. They were making it easy for either one of two reasons: Because they wanted buildings here or meant to burn them soon as she got them finished.

When he got back to the fire again her nailpounders were there with the wagon. One fellow was putting the tent up. Another took care of the horses while the third was unloading the stuff they'd brought out. Joyce, crouching over a new, smaller fire blazing up

55

between stones, was cutting potatoes into a
bacon-greased skillet.

The man who'd been putting the tent up
came over.

The girl looked up with a smile and said,
'Morg, meet Bill Sparks——he's got charge of
the building. You fellows will be seeing quite a
lot of each other during the next several
weeks, so you may as well get acquainted.
Morgan Price,' she told the boss carpenter,
'has full charge of Sloan ranch work and cattle
operations.'

Sparks, Price thought, might know his
hammers and saws but he had more the look
of a barroom bouncer. He had that type's
blocky face and the eyes generally associated
with that sort of livelihood. He surprised Price,
however, by shoving out a hand.

A more unpleasant surprise was in store
when Price took it. The fellow's elephantine
paw closed around Price's fingers with a bone-
crushing grip that would have fetched most
men to their knees in short order. 'Glad to
know you,' Sparks grinned, and closed his fist a
little tighter.

Price didn't try to twist away from it. He
didn't say anything, either, until Sparks let go
of him. He showed then something of the
toughness beaten into him by the years he had
spent punching other men's cattle when he
said with a touch of dry humor, 'I expect you'll
know me better before we're done with this,

56

Sparks,' and went off into the darkness to nurse his hand in private.

*   *   *

After the supper things had been cleared away and Sparks and his companions had rolled into their blankets, Price—back away from the glow of the fire—still hunkered in the shadows with the Winchester across his knees. He had no intention of sleeping. He wasn't trusting that bunch any farther than he could hit them.

His finger joints felt like they'd been run through a wringer. The pain he was entertaining probably colored his thoughts some, but he'd have bet his whole stake there was more to this play than had shown up in the deal yet. Big pay may have hired these fellows as Joyce contended but it was dollars to doughnuts they'd got their orders from Flack.

That handshake hadn't been horseplay. Sparks had done his level best to put Price's gun hand out of commission. An obvious means to an end should Price be foolish enough to get careless.

In the darkness Price's lips shaped an angular smile. There was a cool, earthy dampness in the wind off the river, a thread of wildness in this night smell that coincided with Price's mood. If it was trouble they were after he meant to see they got a bellyfull.

Presently his thoughts got back to the girl

57

again. He didn't pretend to understand her but had to admit he found her exciting. Bullheaded she might be, and uncommonly hard on a man's nerves and temper, still she had an appeal that went beyond looks and figure. It was a quality of imagination perhaps. He didn't know what it was but it had sure got hold of him

Perhaps the mystery surrounding her had more than a little to do with the way he felt about her. He didn't even know what her name was for sure. He didn't, when you got right down to brass tacks, know one durn thing about her that he could swear to—except that she had a heap more courage than sense.

He didn't even know where she had come from!

She'd signed the Orrison's register as E. D. Sloan from El Paso. Yet she had told him on the stage her name was Joyce Darling. He had come across her ad in the Signal City *Star*; yet she had claimed to have written the postmaster from Abilene.

On the stage she had given a variety of impressions. She had seemed too young and friendly to be traveling alone; and, by her clothes, in poor circumstances. The whiskered rancher had thought her a school teacher fresh out of normal school and hunting a job. The mustached romeo had taken her for a credulous fool but, when he'd got too personal, she had put him in his place without any commotion. And, despite her mended clothes, no girl without a bankroll could throw money around the way she'd been doing.

She'd bought this place up for taxes—if you could believe her. Eight years of back taxes on twelve thousand acres wasn't the kind of day wages panned out of a creek bed. And that herd of white-faces! And the crew that was fetching them—*her* crew, she'd called them! And all this lumber for building and the big pay she'd promised—not to mention a ramrod at one-fifty a month!

What did she have—a gold mine?

And why would she buy into this kind of trouble? Anyone with the amount of dough she must have hold of could have done better than this without half trying.

And then he remembered Hi Henry.

She's been through here before, the garrulous stage driver had said. *I can't recollect when nor the wherefors of it, but a man don't fergit a head o' hair like that.*

Price nodded agreement. What was it Henry'd called her? Strawberry roan. Well, it fit, all right; it fit just about as snug as that blue shirt she'd been wearing.

None of which buttered any parsnips. She was here. She was asking for trouble and, once they got set, she'd get all she could handle— and then some. Flack, Archer and Fenwick were not the kind any fellow with all his buttons would aim to go around yelling boo at.

59

Which fetched his thoughts back to another look at himself.

Price scowled and tried flexing his half-paralyzed hand. By gritting his teeth he could close it and open it but it wasn't anything you'd want to reach for a gun with; and it was going to be worse before it got better.

He wished he could figure out what they were up to. Were they planning to jump him some time during the night or was he being softened up for a surprise on the morrow? Anything these birds tried would be brass knuckles and bootheels. They weren't gun men.

But they may not have been intended to try anything. Their whole value to Flack in whatever was brewing might lie wholly in being here, a kind of distraction. A threat, if you please, designed to work on Price's nerves.

He could see their recumbent shapes out-sprawled in the gloom across the glow from the fire. He debated the advisability of piling more wood on, deciding against it. If they were here to make trouble there was no sense postponing it.

The fire burned down and Price caught himself nodding.

When he roused himself again he couldn't see the three carpenters. No moon was looking down and the shadows beyond the dull glow of the embers looked thick enough to cut. But his eyes couldn't cut them; he couldn't tell if those

60

three rannies were over there or not.

He let five minutes slide by without moving a muscle.

A faint scrape of sound, such as one piece of shale might make jostling another, came out of the blackness somewhere off to the left.

Price cocked the rifle.

There were no further sounds.

*   *   *

Red-eyed and bleak of aspect, Price breakfasted in silence.

The carpenters ate with a noisy relish, gabbling among themselves in fine fettle and tossing occasional rough quips at Joyce just as if they had known her since she'd gone around in pigtails.

Price, what times he wasn't glaring at them churlishly, patrolled the place with his glance as though it were a sentry prepared to fire at an instant's notice.

Their feeding finally concluded, tin plates rinsed in the river, Sparks inquired of the girl where she wanted the buildings and she rode off with them to show him.

None of these whippoorwills had fetched their own horses but their boss had got the sorrel ready for Joyce and, without so much as a by-your-leave, had cinched Price's Hamely on the buckskin for himself, telling his two boot-lickers he reckoned they could stick on the team without saddles.

Joyce, endeavoring to settle a stirrup, caught Price's eye and beckoned him over. Before he could get there, however, Sparks shouldered forward and adjusted it for her. 'Nothin' like havin' a good man around,' he grinned.

Joyce gave him a look that would have melted an icicle.

'Oh—Mister Price,' she called brightly. 'When those other three boys show up with the lumber you might ride over with them and show them where to unload it. And, while you're waiting for them, I suppose you might as well get those things put back in the wagon—the foodstuffs, tools and all. We'll move right onto the job.'

She turned her horse around, Spanish style, smiling over Sparks' shoulder. 'And be sure my tent's taken down and packed also.'

Price nodded without comment.

But, after they'd left, he kicked a spade so hard it damned near went in the river.

When their hats had dropped into the green roll of the valley he started checking the supplies. She'd fetched barely enough to last eight people the week out.

He glared at the pile of bright saws and varnished hammers and spat when he came onto three never-used chalklines. But he hoisted the nail kegs into the wagon and packed the raid on the hardware in around them; then he stacked in the groceries and went after the spade. Arranging stubbled cheeks in horrid mimicry of Joyce, he lisped, 'And be sure my tent's taken down and packed also.'

He made sure of it, swearing, and tossed the spade on top of the load along with an ax and two post hole diggers. Then, picking up his rifle, he went over to squat in the shade of a sycamore—not to wait for the lumber, which he felt sure would not arrive, but to try to sort out in his mind how he might deal with the gun crew overdue from Flack.

That looked a pretty large order for a fellow fixed as solo as he was at the moment. He hadn't even got a horse, thanks to that bruiser Sparks' officiousness. But if he could keep out of sight and get the drop on those buggers he might at least have a chance to break up Flack's first play.

CHAPTER SIX

He tried to keep his mind on Flack's probable moves, but this proved hard sledding with that girl all the time scrambling into his thoughts. There was so much about her which eluded understanding. Why, for instance, when he'd been about to line his sights on that sonofagun who'd been throwing lead at them, had she been so set on letting the fellow get away? It wasn't her soft heart.

You could tie a horse on that, all right!

If she had any softness in her he hadn't been able to discover it.

She could turn on the charm, no question about that. But pretty is as pretty does, and what she was figuring to do in this Basin hadn't any prettiness in it. It was a dog eat dog kind of business at best and she was wading right into it with her eyes wide open. Why was she so set on ranching this Basin regardless of the edicts of the Combine or their anger?

And there was that matter of his suggested warning to the crew coming up with her cattle. How could she have been so offhanded about it? By her talk, he thought disgustedly, you might have supposed they'd been discussing the disposal of waste water. Yet she had asked him once, and they had been talking about money, 'Do I look like a fool?'

A thousand registered Herefords represented more dinero than Price had ever seen got together in one lump, and the only plausible reason she could have been so unmoved by their evident danger was a thing he didn't like thinking about.

But he faced it. Grim of eye and dark of scowl, he knew that crew must already have been warned. Must have been told when they were hired the kind of deal they'd be riding into. And, if you accepted this premise, you had to believe she had known from long before she saw Price what forces her arrival would unleash in this country.

If she'd been handy right at that moment he'd have told her what she could do with this job. Since she wasn't he put in the next quarter hour getting in line some of the things he meant to say when he saw her. He became so deeply engrossed in this fashion he heard the bumping and jolting of iron rims on rock for well onto five minutes before the sounds translated themselves into the knowledge that the lumber she'd ordered was just about here.

He sprang up with an oath and took a look through the trees. And sure enough, there it came—three heaping wagonloads of it.

So maybe he'd been wrong about the whole dadblamed business. Maybe, like she'd said, he'd got to worrying too much and, like that old fellow who'd gone after the windmills, was about to find a screw loose.

There were two men with each wagon. The drivers looked like teamsters and the fellows they had with them looked like men used to slinging a hammer. Price—but with his rifle still caught in the crook of an elbow—came out of concealment and strode forward to meet them.

The foremost wagon lurched to a stop.

The guy handling the ribbons of this six-horse hitch stood up and glared down at him. 'You workin' for that woman?'

'Woman?' Price said.

'That redheaded catamount what romped into town wearin' pants an' allowin' she was putting Bar O on the map again!'

'Oh—Sloan,' Price said, nodding.

'Kinda tetched in the head, ain't she?'

Price appeared to be giving this suggestion some thought. 'It's a delicate subject but there are times,' he said finally, 'I'd be inclined to agree with you.'

The driver looked as though he figured maybe Price was 'tetched' too. 'Where's she wantin' this lumber?'

'You see that pile of rock yonder?'

'Dutchwoman Butte.'

'Well, it ain't right there but it's in that direction. Tell you what you do; you point these nags a little east of that butte and I'll ride along with you and show you where to set it down.'

'Climb on,' the driver said, and kicked off the brake.

The sun got higher and hotter and was three hours above the peaks of those flanking eastern mountains when Price and the driver, and the nail-pounder with them, got to where they could see the shapes of Joyce and her companions. They saw the girl look up and wave. The three men with her had their backs turned and were apparently staring toward a buff-colored dust lifting out of the south and coming their way like the breath of a twister.

66

Price said, watching it, 'See if you can shake a little speed from these broncs.'

The driver splashed amber across the tail of a passing roadrunner. 'Ain't nothin' yonder I'm in no tearin' rush to git to.'

'Then let's pretend like there is,' Price drawled, picking up his rifle.

*   *   *

Long before they came up with Joyce's group it became apparent to Price the riders fronting that dust were going to get there first. This heavily loaded wagon was no match for light traveling horsemen, and no amount of cursing or popping of the driver's blacksnake was going to make up the difference.

'Pull up!' Price suddenly shouted.

The perspiring driver slammed on the brake.

Price was over the side before he got the horses stopped, and was swiftly around to the heads of the leaders, cutting the off one out of its harness before the flustered driver realized what he was up to. Price didn't wait for his cursing. Gathering up the cut lines, he leaped onto its back and gave the surprised animal a taste of the steel.

With a squeal of rage the horse bolted. Flattened out along its neck, with left hand gripped in that flying ebony mane, Price encouraged more speed with frequent nudgings of his spurs until the wind was a roar he was unable to hear through. Even so, the dust cloud reached Joyce first, but not by more than about six lengths. Price had to haul the horse back on its haunches in order to set it down without completely overrunning them.

When the dust had cleared enough that he could see what he was up against, he counted five scowling punchers in the glowering group spread out behind Archer. Every one of those rannies had a paw on his pistol and his orbs fixed on Price as though for a couple of coppers he'd as lief blast him loose of this life now as later.

But it was Joyce, not these cow-wallopers, that sent Price's jaw flopping down like a blacksmith's apron.

Any guy is apt to feel a little on the ludicrous side to discover about the time he's getting ready to do his dying he hadn't any call to come a-running in the first place.

Joyce appeared to have the situation very well in hand.

'Oh—Mister Price,' she cooed with all the charm he so blackly remembered, 'have you met Joe Archer? Joe's come over to lend a hand, if we should need one, against the encroachments of Flack and Fenwick. Don't you think that's wonderfully neighborly of him?'

What Price thought was that the way she was rolling those green eyes over Archer the guy probably couldn't tell straight up from down. Price was very well aware he hadn't come over for any such purpose; but you could guess, just by looking at him, that he was finding some pretty likely angles to this notion. With that fatuous smile airing off all his molars Archer looked about ready to sit down with a string of spools.

But he still had wit enough to know which end of the horse took the grass. Scrubbing a hand around his neck he said through the assortment of teeth he was showing, 'I—uh—to tell you the truth—'

'I think, Joe, you've stated it beautifully. I'd no idea Flack and Fenwick were such scoundrels; and I think it's mighty upstanding of you to be willing—'

'But, ma'am, I—'

'I know you men just can't stand being thanked; but you've no idea how much better I'm feeling, just for knowing I've a neighbor like you that I can lean on.'

Archer said, red-cheeked, 'But—'

Joyce, all sweetness and light, smiled reprovingly. ' "By their acts ye shall know them." I hadn't realized till now how true those words were. Please don't lower my good opinion of you, Joe, by belittling the worth of what you've offered to do—and these staunch friends who've volunteered to come with you.'

She gave the 'friends' a smile, too. 'My ramrod, Price, has been trying to make me see the awful depths of depravity into which some men would plunge their very souls for the sake of a few dollars. But I couldn't bring myself to believe, until you opened my eyes, that men reared in the chivalrous traditions of Arizona would attempt to frighten or plunder a lone defenseless girl.'

Price, staring, heard Archer say, 'Well, you've sure got the right of that pair, Miss. Couple of polecats like them would skin a flea for its hide and what lard they could get.'

Joyce sighed with a kind of shudder.

'You're in a bad fix here,' Archer told her. 'Comin' into this grass, like you have, and figuring to build here—'

'It's mine, bought and paid for!'

'That won't make no difference to them kind of fellers.'

'What do you think I should do? Do you honestly feel that I had better sell out?'

Archer, scowling, scratched the back of his neck. 'Ain't nobody around these parts would dast buy it. They've already run one feller out of this Basin.'

Concern, Price thought, sat as comfortable on her as a horse fly snatching a ride on a mule's ear.

But Archer, apparently, considered the show real enough. 'If I was you, Miss,' he said, 'I reckon I'd cross this place off the books and hunt me a spread in some healthier climate. Them skunks is plumb wolf and no two ways

70

about it.'

Joyce looked up at him forlornly.

'Ain't you got no folks?'

'Everything I've got has been sunk into this Basin.'

Archer growled uncomfortably, 'Well now, that's too bad,' and stood frowning.

'Oh,' Joyce said bravely, 'you mustn't let my troubles weigh too heavily on your conscience. I mean, now that you've decided it would be too dangerous to help me—'

'I ain't decided no such thing,' Archer bridled. 'I was just answerin' what you asked me, pointing out the sort of stacked deck you'd be up against with them two. If you're determined to stick I'll certainly do what I can for you.'

'And I thank you for offering. But I don't think I should encourage a neighbor to get into trouble through helping me. After all, you have your own place in this community to think of—'

'Don't you worry about that, Miss. I ain't lettin' no polecats like them two push *me* around! I'd a durned sight rather have you for a neighbor than the kind of plug-uglies Flack an' Fenwick would shove in here.'

'But I shouldn't like to think—'

'Well, don't you do it, ma'am; don't you bother your pretty head with it. You just leave all the thinking to a man that's equipped for it.' He thrust out his jaw and declaimed belligerently, 'Things has sure enough come to a fine pass around here when Joe Archer's got to set back an' watch range hogs run a lone woman right off her own land!'

Joyce's glance would have made any gent stick his chest out.

'Do you suppose,' she asked, smiling up at him trustfully, 'you might leave three or four of your friends overnight here? I mean, to kind of watch out for things while these carpenters are putting my buildings up? I wouldn't want them molested or scared off the job.'

CHAPTER SEVEN

It is one thing good-naturedly to ride along with an unpopular program, and quite another to be asked actively to give one's public support to the business—as a certain young ranchman was belatedly discovering.

Some of the self-righteous glow and easy Christian virtue began to fall out of Archer's widening stare. He showed the look of a man who has been rudely awakened to find all his worst bogies thronging round to be recognized, and shock, indignation and a brightening fear began to leach into his startled expression.

But the poor chump was hooked, Price reflected; Sloan had him spreadeagled over a barrel. He was caught, high and dry, on his own grand importance. No matter what holds Flack and Fenwick had on him, what threats they might seek to pressure him with, he was Joyce's man now or he stood, self-convicted, the most despicable coward this side of El Paso.

Price could sympathize with him—up to a point. But that point was reached where the trail tangled up in Archer's relations with Flack and Fenwick. As he had truly declared, those fellows were wolves, and when you hunt with the wolves any trap is a fair one.

Watching his expression Joyce, with her uncanny knack for putting the finger on a sore spot, said wistfully, 'Of course, Mister Archer, if you're afraid it might weaken your position at Spanish 40 . . .'

Archer showed a parched grin, but he was a more careful man than he had been. Contenting himself with a meager nod he inquired how long she figured to have need of them.

Joyce appeared not to notice this lack of enthusiasm. 'Why, only until our own crew gets in. Would that be asking too much? I don't imagine it will be for more than a couple or three weeks.'

Archer's expression, which had turned a little dour when she had mentioned a crew of her own on the way, displayed a definite strain while he considered that time limit.

But he said gruffly over his shoulder,

73

'Shorty, you and Lippy and Weddin' Ring stick around here awhile and kind of keep your eyes peeled. Don't take no guff off nobody. At the first sign of trouble you get word to me pronto.'

'My!' Joyce assured him, 'that's lifted a load off my mind. Joe, you're a prince! If everyone would be as considerate and cooperative as you've been, I feel sure—'

'That's all right, Miss. You just keep right on feelin' sure and there won't be nothin' you can't get the best of.'

Jerking a nod to his men and touching his hat in Joyce's direction, he swung into his saddle and was preparing to depart when Price's redheaded boss exclaimed with sweet reluctance, 'Oh—Joe! There's just one thing more I kind of wish that you could manage . . .'

Archer's shape went briefly still before the twist of broad shoulders showed a face that might have been hacked out of mountain mahogany.

'Yeah?'

'Do you think it would be too much bother to bring over a little food for them?'

*   *   *

Price waited until the departing Spanish 40 heir and the two who'd gone with him faded into the shimmering dance of the heat waves and then, taking advantage of their mental condition, put the three Archer'd left to work

74

helping Joyce's carpenters get the lumber off the wagons.

The driver whose horse he had cut out of its harness was pawing up the sod like a sore-backed bull; but Price beckoned Joyce aside and said without beating around any bushes, 'You cut the mustard on that deal but just what the hell do we stand to get out of it?'

'We're still breathing, aren't we?'

Price said with his teeth bared, 'You get the brass timepiece for outthinking Archer—what I'm referring to now is those baboons you talked him into leaving. Everything they hear or see will go straight back to Spanish, 40—'

'You figure that's a disadvantage?'

'—and, if it comes to a fight, I'd as soon depend on my two bare hands as put any trust in the likes of them!'

'No one's asking you to put any trust in them.' She considered him curiously. 'Why don't you try using your head for a change?'

Price had some pretty hard thoughts for a man who'd been reared in a Christian environment. He tried breathing through his nose while he counted to fifty but it didn't seem very greatly to improve the situation.

Short of tying a stone around her neck and dropping her into some hole in the river he couldn't see much chance for any peace in the offing. What a fellow really needed when he set out to jaw with her was a good-sized club with a knot on the end of it.

'All right,' he said disgustedly, 'just mark me down as dumb and chew it up some for me.'

'Let's start out with fundamentals. When we came into this country what were we up against?'

'A closed corporation.'

'That's right. Three big outfits—what you might call a "rigged" deck. Only a fool would look to profit playing another man's game. So we introduce our own—'

'And make the mistake of thinking *them* fools.'

'Oh no,' she smiled. 'Just crooks. And, like all crooks, they're suspicious, so we consolidate this weakness by giving it something to feed on.'

'Archer?'

'You don't think Flack and Fenwick will enjoy thinking Archer has come over to us, do you?'

Price snorted. 'He ain't. You've just tangled him up in a trap of words that won't hold him ten seconds when he gets off to think about—'

'So I get him to leave three of his crew here with us. He'll have a hard time talking himself out of that—especially if one of his partners should see them. Flack and Fenwick, while he's shorthanded, might decide to pay him a visit. If they're half as rough as you think they are . . . And it's not going to stop there, either.'

'You called the turn, that time.' Price regarded her dourly, 'All you've said may be true, but that young fool's got a temper. When he finds out what a sap you've made of him—'

She laughed. 'No young man with the looks and build of Joe Archer could ever bring himself to think those facts were lost on a woman—and isn't he heir to Spanish 40? Besides he's ambitious.'

'You know too damned much about men!' Price growled.

'You're not jealous, Morg, are you?'

Those laughing green eyes rubbed his fur the wrong way and he strode off without answering.

Sparks, with the seat of his pants on a rock, was chucking hard looks at Archer's perspiring punchers when Price, hands on hips, stopped a couple feet away from him. 'You just admiring the view or taking a siesta?'

Sparks' blocky face looked up at Price insolently. 'I'm not workin' for you so don't let it worry you—'

Price slammed a clenched fist against the side of Sparks' face and the boss carpenter went off the rock heels over elbows.

He came up looking wild enough to twist bar iron but a glance down Price's gun snout took a lot of it out of him. 'We got no room in our wagon for a loafer's blankets. If you expect to eat around here you'll put in a day's work. Now grab a saw and get at it.'

Something the boss carpenter read in Price's eyes must have convinced him that right now this was no guy to monkey with. Looking meaner than gar soup thickened with tadpoles he snatched up an apron and started rounding up his crew.

Price went over to where Archer's cowhands were lifting the last of the lumber off the last wagon. They had observed his little set-to with Sparks and watched his approach with inscrutable faces.

'When you get done with this,' he said, 'go over and ride herd on that horse stock. I don't want none of those birds taking off without my say so.'

The bowlegged fellow Archer had called Wedding Ring rubbed a hand on his pants and said dubiously, 'Y'mean them carpenters?'

'That'll do for a brand until I find something better.' He stepped across to where the punchers' horses were browsing, hauled a rifle off its saddle and took a look at the magazine. This was a highpowered job using the same caliber cartridge as the gun which had tried to cut him down from the mesa. But these were centerfire shells and they weren't marked like the one Price carried in his pocket.

Thrusting the rifle back in its scabbard he repeated the process with those on the other broncs. The three rifles were identical and so were their cartridges.

Taking the third rifle with him Price went up to the blanket-rigged awning under which Sparks sat industriously scratching figures on a short piece of board.

Sparks made out to ignore him.

Price, taking a look at the figures, wrenched the board from Sparks' grip and sailed it off in the broomweed. A rageful snarl ripped its way across the roan of Sparks' features and he came lunging erect, swelling up like a carbuncle.

Price said—and in that quiet his words fell distinct as gunshots—'You're not being fed to doodle. Sloan's paying for the best and she's expecting to get it. When she don't somebody's—'

'Hell with you! I'm gettin' out—'

'Oh, no, you're not. You came out here to put up buildings and you'll be staying right here until you get the job done.'

Sparks had been put together on the gorilla pattern and looked physically to have a clear advantage over Price, but he was not used to being stood up to. The conviction in Price's tone rattled him and the unyielding look of Price's stare backed him down; and he turned balefully away muttering threats and imprecations.

Price, glancing around for the teamsters, found them dwindling specks on the homeward-bound trail that snaked up from the bench through the blur of ash and sycamore obscuring the approach to the bridge above Thief River.

He beckoned one of the Spanish 40 boys.

'Just this side of where you see those specks you'll find a loaded wagon. Light out with that team and fetch it over here.'

The man, looking about to protest, appeared to think better of the notion when he examined Price's face. He rasped a hand across his jowls and went off to catch up the team.

A couple of minutes later one of the other punchers nudged him and, following the direction of the man's scrinched stare, he saw a dust between the river and a notch in those rimming mountains. The leisurely horseman making it looked to be not over a mile away and there wasn't much doubt but that this camp was his destination.

'Slim Piggott,' Archer's cowhand informed him. 'Rides strayman for Gill.'

'And who's Gill?'

'Flack's range boss at Anvil.'

Price, remembering the wedge-faced man in the black Texas hat he had seen in the Orrison's bar two nights ago, said: 'Got cat's eyes over a shape like a bed slat?'

The Spanish 40 man ran a very thoughtful tongue along the corrugated bottoms of a number of upper molars. 'If you ain't in no tearin' rush to git planted it might pay you to be careful where you sling that hand of chin music.'

Price, remotely smiling, watched Gill's strayman reach the river, watched him stare across awhile before he put his roan horse into it.

Then Price picked up the rifle.

'All right, Shorty. Drift along to the end of those planks and drop your bottom where it won't get in the way if any lead should get to whistling.'

'Aw, he won't start nothin—not with all these jaspers standin' round.'

'I ain't figuring to have you start nothing, either. Get over there now and step lively.'

*   *   *

Slim Piggott, coolly anchoring a knee around the horn of his saddle, looked operations over with a frank curiosity, finally saying to Shorty, 'Your boss is kinda takin' a lot for granted, ain't he?'

Shorty shrugged, and Price said, 'Who invested you with authority to go around asking questions?'

'Who's this?' Piggott said to Shorty, jerking a negligent thumb in Price's direction.

'Bar O boss.'

'Bar O? That's a laff! There ain't been no damn Bar O in this country since the Combine run that sodbuster off.'

Shorty said uncomfortably, 'One here now, it looks like.'

Anvil's strayman spat contemptuously. 'The only free ground around here for squatters—

an' their friends—is the kind we bury them nailed-up pine boxes in. You tell this greener,' he said sneeringly to Shorty, 'he better haul his freight while he can git out in one piece.'

Price set down his rifle and stepped over to Piggott's stirrup.

'Maybe you feel big enough to tell me that yourself?'

Piggott swung a booted foot at Price's jaw but wasn't quick enough. Swaying aside Price caught it and twisted the strayman out of the saddle. He lit hard on one shoulder and then Price had hold of him. Jerking the gun from Slim's holster he pulled the man upright and, spinning him round, slapped him back of an ear. The fellow's legs folded and he went down for the count.

'Fetch a hatful of water,' Price tossed at the gaping Shorty; but the strayman came out of it before the cowboy returned, rolling over and coming groggily onto an elbow.

Price took the water and threw it over him anyway. 'You can tell that guy back at Anvil you been down in the dust and you know what it tastes like. And you can tell him from me that if I catch any more of his bully boys over here he's going to find out what it tastes like himself. Now get on that crowbait and start making tracks.'

*　　　*　　　*

Price, after watching Piggott splash across the river, was prowling the black-and-roan dust in search of the stray man's flung-away pistol when Joyce came up from the direction of the lake.

In the snug fitting shirt, against the green and yellow broomweed with the blue sky beyond it tastefully flecked with fleecy clouds, she made a picture to get into a man, a sight to call up his brashness.

'Morg,' she said, stopping close to him, 'the way you handled that fellow was a joy to behold. I want you to know I'm proud of you.'

Price, never bothering to so much as glance around, kept on with his hunting as though completely immune to the witchery of her presence.

A faint shadow washed across the greenness of her stare, but the red lips did not lose their smile and she said in that husky voice he found so fetching, 'You can't imagine, of course, how much it means to me to have Bar O respected. What you did will give those—'

'Kid stuff!' Price snarled bitterly, and flung around with an outraged stare. 'Don't think I'm proud of a thing like that. It won't scare those fellows, only make 'em mad—'

'Good!' Joyce's glance brightened wonderfully. 'The madder they get the better I'll like it!'

Price shook his head. 'You're crazy, Sloan.'

'Because I want them to be riled?' She smiled a bit grimly. 'Maybe I am . . . it doesn't much matter. We'll never get the best of those fellows until we get them mad enough to make a mistake.'

'I thought you came here to ranch—'

'That's your whole trouble. You think too much, Morgan.'

'And all you want,' Price said angrily, 'is some big dumb ox that will do what he's told and not give a damn whether school keeps or not!'

Her green eyes laughed up at him, openly provocative.

Price, glaring at her, hesitated. But the exciting sensual lines of her mouth and the curves filling out that tight shirt suddenly proved too much for him to longer resist; and he caught her to him, hungrily kissing her roughly.

It was like the top of the world had come off.

She was breathless when she pushed him away and there was a lot more color in her cheeks than there had been. She brushed a lock of tawny hair back from her forehead. 'At least you can't say now that you haven't been paid.'

Slamming clenched hands deep into his pants pockets Price turned on his heel and it was ten minutes later before he missed Bill Sparks. He looked all around and then he grabbed hold of Shorty. 'You seen that damned carpenter?'

'Which one's that?'

'That big burly bruiser—the one that looks like an ape.'

'Oh, him! No, I haven't.' He separated himself from Price by eight or ten steps and picked up a piece of lumber. 'There's a horse missin', too.'

CHAPTER EIGHT

Old man Archer, who still counted himself able to know right from wrong and to abide by the consequences, sat ramrod-straight on Spanish 40's back porch, a pair of crutches beside him and a cold pipe gripped in his tobacco-stained teeth. The cook had padded out and fetched him matches half an hour ago but still he sat on, the unlit cob forgotten as his bright and bitter glance, crossing the tangle of ravine and river, probed the hundred-foot ponderosas which obscured the Basin trail.

For eight years that Basin, and the fool who'd tried to farm it, had corroded all his thinking until the place now stood a symbol for all the mistakes he had ever made, and he cursed the damned bullheadedness which had taken his son back into it.

He had seen long ago that he'd been nothing but a pawn in that unholy alliance a moment's greed had pushed him into, but this did not in any way alter the fact of his support, or the worth of his given word. If Flack and Fenwick had made up their minds to drop Spanish 40 from the roll call of sharers, recriminations would not dig any turnips. Nor all of Joe's floppymouthed bluster.

Grab the Basin, indeed!

Archer scowled and hitched his chair a little closer to the pine facing nailed across the front of the porch with the intention of keeping the rain out. He tucked the folds of a rug more firmly about his leg against the encroaching chill of twilight and damned the bronc which had immobilized him.

How well he could recall the mulish obstinacy of that plow chaser and those apparently innocuous moves by which the poker-faced Flack had gained control of the squeeze-play partnership which had been the nester's undoing. He thought about Fenwick who was just a cheap crook and wondered when Flack would get around to Spanish 40, entertaining no illusions about his ability to protect it. The man was like a black spider.

The sun had flopped below the crags and its last cerise glow was practically gone from the hills when, with an irascible grunt, Archer observed the dark shapes of horsemen moving out of the pines and dropping into the ravine for their splash across the river. He counted but three and his stony look tightened.

He sat stiffly in the gathering gloom and

listened to the sounds of men unsaddling, and finally got up and hobbled into the house. He chunked a couple of pine knots onto the built-up hearth of the Indian fireplace and let himself down into a leather-backed chair with the bitterness of a man who has assessed his limitations.

When his son came into the room Archer said with the voice of judgment, 'Where are the other three boys you took with you?'

Joe said defensively, 'They're not dead, if that's what you're gettin' at. I left them to keep an eye on things.'

'What things?'

'You'll be surprised to know we've got neighbors again. There's a girl moved onto that grass. Claims she's bought up the land for taxes. Got carpenters in there and a range boss with her and a crew on the way here now with her cattle.'

'She's a fool and they'll run her out,' Archer growled.

'Sure they will—if we let 'em.'

Archer bent on his son an uncharitable glance. 'You taken leave of your senses?'

'It's the chance, of a lifetime—'

'Say a chance to get buried and I'll agree with you.'

'If I'm goin' to be buried,' Joe Archer declared loudly, 'I'll do something besides sit here an' wait for it! You know well as I do Flack's set to freeze us out—first the Basin and then this place. We got a chance here to get a little run for our money and, by the Eternal, I mean to have it! I'm going to throw our weight on the side of that girl—'

'You'll do nothing of the sort. I'm still owner of this place and I'm a part of that Combine till they chuck me out—'

'They'll chuck you out, all right, if you give them the chance!'

'I gave them my word when they went after that nester. It's not a thing that I'm proud of but I'll not take it back—'

'And what has it got you? What's it got me but a kick in the pants! If you think I'm goin' to sit around on my fanny and watch that tinhorn take over this country you were never more mistaken.'

'What do you think you can do?'

'I've let her see what she's up against. I haven't told her yet that half those carpenters she's rounded up are on Flack's payroll. I've got Lippy and Shorty and Weddin' Ring watchin' them and watchin' for anything else Flack may try to pull. This situation's made to order. If she's got any kind of crew at all, her bunch and ours have got a chance to keep those highbinders out of there, and if they do—'

'You think a properly grateful girl is going to take your hand in marriage and make you a present of that Basin?'

'You know any better way to get it?'

There was something unsparing in the look the old man gave him, something piteous too in the knowledge of his own impotency. Then he set his unlit pipe on the floor beside the hateful tokens of it and said in a blunt and growling tone: 'And how are you going to protect Spanish 40? You've got five men and, even with her crew, you'll need every one of them—'

'Let them have this place. They're goin' to get it anyway. When I've built up enough on Basin grass I'll take it back again, and maybe Fenwick's place along with it.'

Old man Archer said without bothering to look at him, 'Ambition's a pretty powerful thing when there are brains to go with it, and a damn foolish thing when there is nothing behind it but a lot of hot air.'

Joe Archer flushed. 'You could be wrong about me.'

'I've been wrong about a lot of things, but not about you. You're a scheming, conniving, egotistical bastard, and I'll tell you where you are going to wind up—on a slab in that damned back room at Creighton's Furniture.'

*   *   *

Price was in a foul mood when he went tearing out of the Bar O camp on a Spanish 40 horse shortly after discovering the boss carpenter had rolled his cotton.

He didn't give a hoot about the fellow's professed ability or even about the things he might blab should he reach Sunflower. Anything Sparks had discovered worth telling, Flack would soon be hearing from his manhandled strayman.

Price was going after Sparks for whatever salutary effect it might have on the rest of those nail-pounders Joyce had hired, but the buckskin horse was the prime cause of this chase. Price didn't want to lose that hide.

He guessed in its youth it must have been a humdinger; it was still a fast traveler with a great deal of bottom. A Billy horse by the looks of it, perhaps with a cross or two from old Steel Dust. He wasn't much interested in the animal's bloodline ancestry. Price's thinking had taken another tack entirely.

There was something about this ten-year-old gelding which persuaded Sloan's ramrod the horse might have a value far in excess of its intrinsic worth.

He had not forgotten the way it had fetched him onto the burned-over site of the ranch's former buildings. Nor its Terrapin brand. Nor the way he had twice caught the girl staring at it. Unless Price was ready to be bored for the simples that horse was a link with something he figured out was going to bear looking into.

The sun was pretty well down by the time he reached the road and went clattering over the bridge, but he could see Sparks' dust and urged his mount to overtake it.

He understood before they'd gone a mile he wasn't going to catch up with anything short of Sunflower. The buckskin already had gained too much ground and was still pulling away when Price quit using the spurs on his own bronc. This jughead he'd borrowed from the phlegmatic Shorty didn't have no more bottom than a shotgunned bucket.

Price took his time after that and darkness overtook him long before he reached the town. When he was still a half mile from its lamp-lighted windows he halted Shorty's horse and dropped the reins over the horn. Drawing out his gun he spun the cylinder a couple of times and dropped the weapon back in leather. As he'd remarked some time ago, Price was no professional smoke-poler, but he reckoned he could make the thing talk if he had to.

Sparks, if he had this deal sized up right, would go straight to Flack.

Price's thoughts tacked carefully over the angles. It could make considerable hay for Sloan in the fight shaping up over Bunchgrass Basin if he could walk right into Flack's headquarters and take Bill Sparks away from him. And it could also get Price jailed or killed.

He decided to forget about Sparks and concentrate on the horse.

He reckoned he would find it racked in front of the Oirison, and he did. With six or eight others. It was in the center of the bunch and looked to have its reins securely knotted about the hitch rail.

He was not quite sure why he figured that horse so important and rather irritably wondered if it were mostly because Bill Sparks had chanced to take it. Convenience might have decided Sparks' choice, or nothing more than the animal's deceitfully youthful appearance. There were a number of reasons why Sparks might have taken it having no relation to the brand it was packing. But Sparks had also borrowed it that morning and, of the seven horses available, had peculiarly chosen to light out on the buckskin.

Piano sound was coming from the bar's open windows, talk and clack of chips and the tinkling of touched glasses; but there was something about this street which Price abruptly didn't care for. It looked a lot too dark for one thing and very much too quiet now he'd got around to noticing it. At this hour there had ought to be more people moving about, more squatting punchers exercising their talking talents.

He thought back to the night he'd come in on the stage. Been an hour or so later but there'd been lights in Mosher's Hardware and in the furniture store across the way and in the now darkened Mercantile which flanked the Orrison's farther side. The only pool of radiance within a hundred feet of Price was the light coming through the bar windows and falling directly across that line of hitched horses.

Price took a scrinched look at his hole card and caught the sour smell of beer and the ranker stench of someone's canned garbage and leaned forward a moment on the swell of the pommel for a thoughtful appraisal of these darkened store fronts.

He felt cold air flow across the sweat on his neck and the tightness of his stomach muscles cramped a little tighter. He felt a wildness in this quiet and a stalking sense of danger. And then the pressure of his knees telegraphed the gray horse forward; and it was sidling into the bunch of racked horses, forcing passage between the buckskin and a cantankerous sorrel tied next to it when Price's glance caught a stirring in the shadows heavily piled against the front of Mosher's Hardware.

Tension crept along Price's ridgebone.

A couple of bronc stompers who'd been arguing a few doors back when Price rode past had managed to fade completely. Two places which had shown lights then now were black as the Queen of Spades, and he knew in this moment that with all his tall thinking he'd been careless enough to sell Flack short.

And he knew one other thing—that without he could immediately produce some kind of miracle, in a matter of seconds he'd be too dead to skin.

But Shorty, too, had outfoxed him. On this puddinfooted plowhorse he had no possible chance of getting out of the glare from those uncurtained windows before some trigger artist handed him a harp.

He did the next best thing and dropped out of the saddle, diving under the buckskin's belly with the scream of a cougar just as gunflame tore from the shadows of Mosher's porch.

The terrified broncs all about him started pitching and a rifle's sharp crack-crack commenced a pounding from the Mercantile and, in the midst of all this racket, the street door of the bar was flung wide open, giving additional light for Flack's gunhawks to shoot by.

But in that kicking plunging maelstrom of horseflesh Price, with his head down, wasn't easy to locate; and, abruptly, with a rending groan of splintered wood, the tie rail was torn from its uprights. The horses, tied short, took the rail along with them as shod hoofs pounded the boardwalk fronting the Orrison.

One of those slugs, intended for Price, struck the far left horse and it went down like an anchor and swung the rest around before its stretched reins snapped. The right end of the pole crashed through the bar's curtained windows, taking glass, drapes and collapsed frames with it and Price, with one hand wrapped around the horn of his Hamely, wrecked Flack's crystal chandelier with a

94

couple of lucky shots.

There were other lamps in there—two or three anyway—but they didn't light the street the way that chandelier had done; and Price hauled himself into the saddle as his remuda, still tied fast to the gyrating hitch pole, prepared to line out for the open range. But as they wheeled past the Orrison lights flared up in the unshaded windows of the building next beyond it and Price, giving Flack more credit than perhaps the man had coming, imagining lights might blaze from each dark building as he reached it, swung the buckskin hard to the right, forcing the others with it. And they tore down the street snapping one awning post right after another, leaving that whole row of building fronts obscured behind a wreckage of collapsed roofing.

The pandemonium was terrific.

Just as the bank swung into view a group of gun-waving horsemen bulged into the street ahead of them and Price, yanking off the buckskin's bridle, spun the gelding free and whirled it into a trash-littered alley between the two nearest buildings.

But either the whole town was now aroused or Flack had left nothing to chance. A window slammed up just behind Price's head and a gun poured whining lead past his shoulders and the buckskin squealed and turned a corner with its back humped like a half drowned cat.

But it had once been well trained, as Price

had already noticed, and he soon had it answering the signals of his knees. A plank corral loomed through the murk and, beyond it, the incomplete shape of a barnlike building. Some chord of memory vibrated and Price realized he was staring at the dark back end of the Copper State Feed & Livery.

Behind him, through a rising cacophony of clattering hoofs, someone shouted. Price jumped the buckskin left and then forward in a driving run for the back of that stable.

He heard lead biting deep into the planks of the corral and presently they were rounding it, coming into the livery's runway. The black maw of Price's objective looked less than a good rope's throw away when he abruptly stopped the animal behind the timbers of a chute.

These back lots he'd been traversing narrowed rapidly beyond him where the rocky shanks of Old Baldy pinched into the piled-up shadows stacked against the backs of the town's business establishments. The thought was now in Price's mind that getting him into that stable might be just what Flack wanted.

But, even as he hung there, hesitating, the thick gloom beyond it was thinned by the appearance of a lantern in the hand of a frock-coated gambler. The man had stepped out of the blacksmith shop and was settling the lantern's bail in a hook fixed above the smith's doorway. Back of him someplace a man called a warning and the gambler's gaunt shape twisted out of Price's vision; and then a bullet kicked dust between the buckskin's hind feet and it went into the air as a second slug drilled a pine plank with the sound of a hornet.

If Price could have got his hands on a saddle gun he might have put out that lantern. But all he had was his pistol and a horse that was just about fed up with shooting. Gripping its barrel with his knees and slapping his hat across its rump, Price sent the snorting gelding buckjumping into the open.

The horsebackers splitting up to round the corral spotted him at once against the light from that lantern. Gun thunder banged against the backs of the buildings and muzzle lights winked from the trash piled between them. One slug tore through the sweat-wet cloth of Price's shirt and the gelding, agony lifting it onto hind legs, screamed like a woman and suddenly fell apart under him.

CHAPTER NINE

Price, kicking boots free of oxbows, jumped; but his feet wouldn't hold him. He was whipped around like a rag in a gale and fetched up against a fence post hard enough to tilt it. He had no recollection of falling but when he pulled his face up out of the dust the darkness above him was being ripped by blue whistlers and the ground underneath him was shaking like crazy to the approaching thunder of ironshod hoofs.

He tried to push himself upright but the pain was too much for him. He tried to get back his breath and his bellows felt as though they were being fried on a stove lid. And he was like that, not much caring if he ever saw Joyce again, when a lift of his glance took in a blur of trousered legs rushing toward him through the dim lemon shine of the smith's distant lantern.

He wriggled over on his stomach and thought he was about to heave up everything he had in it when a pair of hands caught him, back of the shoulders and dragged him into the barn's smelly blackness.

The familiar odors of hay and horse dung brought him around to where he was able to realize the fellow had let go and was now crouched above him, breath held, listening. Then the advancing gleam of a knee-high lantern pushed an elongated shadow grotesquely over the floor, and outside someone said, 'We got the goddam horse!'

Saddle gear creaked and through a tinkling of spur chains a voice growled harshly, 'What you waitin' on? Fan out an' start huntin—he can't of got far. You, Slank, take Freel's light there an' have a look through that barn.'

'No use wastin' your time on this place,' the man beside Price declaimed, reluctantly moving his weight toward the speaker. 'He never come in here.'

'How you know he never?'

'What you think I been settin' here for with this rifle?'

Price, hardly able to believe his own hearing, came up on an elbow and twisted his head around. He took a long look at that shape in the doorway and actually pinched himself to find if he were dreaming.

But he wasn't. The man was Sparks.

Sparks sticking his neck out to save Price's bacon!

About as likely a thing as pounding sand down a rat hole, Bar O's ramrod told himself uncomfortably. But he was in no condition to turn his nose up at anything.

Glad enough for the respite the pseudo carpenter's game was gaining him, Price crawled warily behind some sacked feed and slipped off his boots. Then, with boots in one hand and gun in the other, he started cautiously toward the dim oblong of what he naturally supposed to be the barn's street door.

In working toward this objective he stayed as close as he was able to that musty near wall, hoping in this manner to reduce the chances of discovery which must certainly follow should he be sighted against that opening. It was a nerve-racking process by reason of the oddments of gear someone had pegged to the wall and scattered with sacked grains along its joint with the floor. A lot of these things he couldn't see and had to feel his way about them, aware that he might stumble over something any moment or bring a horse collar down and give the whole show away.

Nor dared he risk looking back lest his face be caught in the shine of that lantern, for it was obvious enough now the fellow questioning Sparks wasn't figuring to take Sparks' word for anything. He had the tone of a suspicious character and appeared to be invested with considerable authority.

But Price wasn't giving much heed to their jawing.

He was uneasily conscious of having done something wrong, remembering enough of this barn from his previous visits to know that ere now he should have reached the box stalls flanking either side of the runway between front and rear.

He bitterly cursed beneath his breath.

No chance of turning back now. By the sounds they were making that rough-voiced gent had put more than one man to the business of finding whether Price were here or not. And he would not be forgetting that front entrance, either. Or this passage Price was traveling.

Price pushed on, not entirely abandoning caution, but giving more attention to the need to get out of this. The opening ahead of him was plainer now and it was definitely an opening for he could catch the wink of stars.

Considerably encouraged, Price twisted a look over his shoulder, encountering nothing but darkness behind him.

Wasting no time in fruitless speculation, he pulled on his boots and hurried into the gray gloom ahead of him. The blessed feel of night air flowed against his damp cheeks but its relief was shortlived in the irony of what he had come to. At first his appalled mind would not take in the bitter knowledge but the cold feel of wire was very real to his touch. And the restive stamping of hoofs carried final conviction.

Instead of reaching an exit he had come to the out-of-doors cage of a stallion. A bronc pen made from woven hog wire.

The door was made of wire stretched across an iron frame and he could open it—but to what purpose? Any horse kept inside as ruggedly built a place as this was either one of two things—damned valuable or damned dangerous.

Even as Price stood eyeing it the stealthy scuff of a boot sole came out of the blackness back of him and the dim shape of the horse flung its head up with challenging whistle of breath that left no doubt of its status, in Price's mind at least.

A dozen wild thoughts made their rush through his brain and were as swiftly discarded. To go into that pen might prove more deadly than capture. Price had ridden his share of rough ones and knew from experience what a bad bronc was like; and there'd be no place to hide in there anyway, nor any chance to climb out, for the top of the pen was wired also. He might jerk open the door and jump aside in the hope the horse would go for whoever was trying to slip up behind him, but if there was more than one man in that blackness loosing this horse would avail him little. In these unfamiliar surroundings in this cul-de-sac he had so hopefully walked into, every advantage would be on the side of his enemies. They would give him one shot, and the instant his hammer drove flame from the barrel they would drill him; and he had no guarantee they would not drill him anyway.

He dropped his pistol back in leather. They'd be waiting for him now, grinning in those black and impenetrable shadows, waiting for him to try to return the way he'd come. Waiting until his foot, like that other, declared his whereabouts. Then the guns would speak and that would be the end of him.

Simple and effective. A man shot attempting to get away with another's horse.

He put out his left hand, feeling along the door's edge until his fingers found the hasp and very quietly drew its bolt. From some other part of the stable he could hear muted sound of the continuing search, a practical gesture designed to reassure and coax him out of the frying pan into the fire of Flack's alerted artillery.

His lips thinned a little. His narrowed eyes watched the horse, studying its action as it came a few steps toward him, ears flattened. He eased the door open a fraction, standing well to one side, and the stallion stopped moving and stood head up, ears forward, watching it.

Price put weight on the iron frame, testing it, back muscles tightening in expectation of some sound which would send hammers banging against the heads of chambered cartridges.

But no sound came and, satisfied, Price climbed it, got both feet on the ledge of its tip and gingerly straightened to full height next the hinge.

The horse had moved back a little making it hard for Price to see him except as a blacker blur against the gray gloom. And he was pawing again now, snorting softly.

Price wasn't kidding himself about anything. He understood all too well what kind of fix he was in. He didn't have the chance of a fly on gummed paper but he would have a lot less if he was still here come daylight.

He pulled the slack from his belt and could feel his knees shaking. He flexed them slightly, half crouching; stalling, he thought contemptuously.

Faint heart never filled a flush. This was neck meat or nothing and, hauling in his breath, he sank the most of his weight on the doorpost and with his right leg eased the gate all the way open, willing the damned horse to see it.

He needn't have wasted any worry on that score.

The horse saw it all right and came off the ground with a piercing scream. He went up on hind legs and came three jolting strides closer, snuffing through flared nostrils. Then he wheeled about wildly, took several dancing steps and, head twisting shakily, loosed another shrill scream and pounded a front hoof.

Exciting whispers floated out of the shadows behind Price and he knew that in a moment they'd be onto his game.

He fumbled a cartridge from his shell belt and threw it underhand, catching the bronc on the rump. He came about as though on springs. His head disappeared between his front legs and his hind legs came within a hand's breadth of the pen's wired top. The third time up those shod hoofs ticked it and someone back of Price cursed. The stallion's head came up with rolling eyes and he was in a dead run by the time he reached the gate.

'It's the feller that knows how to die standing up that keeps a-coming,' Price muttered, and flung himself onto the animal's back.

The stallion squealed with rage and threw hind feet in the air without breaking its stride or slowing down in the slightest. But Price, with both hands locked in its mane and big-rowelled spurs locked under its belly, stayed aboard; and then the guns started banging from both sides of the passage and the bronc's shoulder shook one high yell from one of Flack's smoke-polers who hadn't moved fast enough.

Buck-jumping and squealing, the horse tore through the muzzle-lighted murk like a bat out of Carlsbad. Shouts and curses lashed its wake and more shouts came out of the blackness ahead of them and, abruptly, the brute swapped leads and went hard left around an unseen corner and someone dead ahead yelled, 'Shut the goddam doors!' and was frantically firing when the horse crashed into him.

Price felt a shudder ripple through the bronc's hide and knew it had been hit; and now, through the pounding gloom, he could see the black shapes of men springing across the gray opening of the barn's front entrance.

He had heard the back doors slam and knew if they got these shut they would have him where the hair was short. Flattening himself still closer against the sweat-wet neck of the terrified outlaw, he yelled like a Comanche and, snatching his pistol, triggered three slugs above those bobbing hats driving toward the doors.

Two of them wilted out of sight like clay pigeons. The others scattered like quail but spun, firing and cursing, as the snorting stallion with Price still aboard lunged past the doors they hadn't managed to slam shut.

Price came out of that barn hellity larrup. But quick as the horse got enough slack to see with, to know he was out in the windy open with no lead plums flying round within hearing, he split down the seams and came apart in short order.

Price did his best to keep the critter's head up but the bronc boiled over anyway, sunfishing, slatting his sails and pretty generally appearing to try to crack himself in two. When he could see he wasn't going to make it he rushed Price at a fence corner, leaving a stretch of hide behind when Price, at the very last instant, snatched up his leg and let the stallion rap his ribs against it. He moaned and swapped ends like a turpentined cat, and wrinkled up his spine until you'd have thought he'd warped it permanent. He actually managed to get shed of Price once by flinging his hind end over his head. But when he lunged to his feet again Price was back of his withers, still outguessing him, still fanning him flank and shoulder with that detestable floppy piece of man-smelling felt.

Then the guns started breaking up the night again. The bronc postponed his feud with Price and got down to the business of making

106

farapart tracks. He even so far forgot his grudge against humans that ere they'd quit the main drag in that flying leap left past the bank's creaking sign and a line of flapping wash, he was taking Price's guidance and thinking nothing of it.

*   *   *

They were crossing the rattling planks of the bridge above Thief River's gorge when Price got his first whiff of woodsmoke. There wasn't much left of the wind by this time but what little there was was coming out of the south on a line that must have crossed Bar O's camp getting up here.

It was a worrying thought because the smell favored pine and the only pine around there was what had come out from town on those highchargers' wagons.

Price spent several moments looking grimly at the sky but there were no flares in it, no light at all which didn't come from the stars. Yet he kept sniffing the air, and the horse did too, tossing its head and blowing like its nose had got filled up with rollers.

All Price could be sure of was that willow hadn't made that smell, nor cottonwood, nor broom. And the horse was showing signs of not caring for that pungence any more than Price himself did.

He was a powerful brute with a fast set of

heels and what a rangebred man would be apt to call 'real bottom.' And, as Price had suspected, he had once been well trained, as gait and manners coming up here had proved beyond doubting. Though Price had sat his tantrums out and he had afterwards accepted guidance, it was plain he didn't mean for Price to build anything on that basis. For now, as though to remind him they were not friends by a long shot yet, he suddenly reached bared teeth around and tried to catch hold of Price's nearest leg.

Price slapped him across the face with his hat and sent him down the rough shelving trail that dropped to the bench through ash and sycamore, slowing him as they climbed the embankment for a sharp and continuing scrutiny of the mesa's black rim where it was limned against stars. And, on the bench, Price pulled him up to listen.

But they caught no sound of travel, no sign of an alien presence.

They pushed south at a walk by tacit agreement and the man's worrying mind picked up Bill Sparks again and pushed him around as an entomologist might some unfamiliar bug.

Why had Sparks pulled him into that barn and told such a whopper to the rest of Flack's understrappers? Could he have had a change of heart after quitting Sloan's camp and, seeing to what use Flack had put that

108

buckskin, been trying to make amends for his part in the business?

It could be so, Price decided, but was not prepared to buy it. Neither Sparks' looks nor previous actions lined up to any such answer.

Could he have decided to swap sides on account of the girl?

It seemed a heap more likely he'd been bidding for the chance of fetching Price in singlehanded. For kudos, cash or both. At least this theory had the merit of geeing with demonstrable facts.

Sparks had been Flack's man when he had quit Bar O. He'd dug for Sunflower on the buckskin, and it looked like giving too much to coincidence to imagine his choice to have been a thing of blind luck. It had not been chance which had darkened that street of all light save the blaze which had shone on that hitch rack. And, after Sparks had done his good turn for the day, pointing it up with a lie for good measure, how had Flack's crowd so quick got onto Price's whereabouts? Only Sparks could actually have known where he had dropped Price. Only Sparks could have seen him crawl behind that sacked grain. Yet some had known where he was and had been right on his tail while the rest of Flack's gunhawks had been searching the stable.

Price, deciding to turn his mind out for a spell, became increasingly aware of the taint of burned wood. The farther south they got the stronger the smell became and Price's means of locomotion was showing about ready to act up again.

Price tightened the grip of his knees about its barrel and, uncomfortably aware he might have need of it shortly, replaced the spent shells in his pistol with fresh ones.

He had intended, while in town, to lay in some ammunition and to order more stuff in the grub line. But Flack's smoke-polers had allowed him no time for running errands, and an extension of this thought abruptly claimed his whole attention.

Suppose this burnt wood smell was coming from Spanish 40! Flack's crew at Anvil, after the report of that strayman, may very well have dropped over to Archer's for a visit.

It was while he was considering the various avenues this opened that the stallion made its second bid for Price's leg. Price indignantly slammed his boot against its jaw. Time he got the horse straightened out they weren't, he figured, very far from camp. He could see the black obelisk of Dutchwoman Butte like a solitary finger jutting into the sky; and dawn was not more than two hours off when they passed it.

He went forward even more slowly now, aware of and concerned about the possibilities of ambush. He rode with one hand on the butt of his six-shooter and one eye watching the ears of his mount.

There was no light coming from the camp at all, nor any doubt now in Price's mind where that fire had been. The air was rank with its smell and with the odor of blood. So much so that the bronc between Price's knees snorted nervously with alarm and gave all the indications of preparing to bolt.

For about forty seconds Price had his hands full. Abandoning caution then, he lifted his voice.

Joyce's answering call came dispiritedly back. She was alone with her arms about her drawn-up knees and her back propped against what was left of the cottonwood. There was nothing else around she could have put it against.

CHAPTER TEN

Price could almost feel sorry for her after he'd looked around. There was a completeness to what had been done here—a stark, cold-blooded thoroughness recalling the devastation which had driven that sodbuster out. Joyce hadn't any fields or any orchard to lay waste, but nothing she had fetched here had been spared.

Every horse, including the team and the mounts of Archer's cowhands, had been slaughtered. All that high-priced lumber had gone up in smoke. The wagon, and everything Price had packed into it, had been reduced to ashes. There wasn't a carpenter in sight and, as that dull gray light which comes just ahead of dawn made the ground about him plainer, he could see where the Spanish 40 boys had set off south afoot.

He poked a hand toward their tracks. 'Looks like Archer's help didn't amount to much.'

Joyce shrugged, not bothering to lift her head. 'We were taken by surprise.'

When Price kept his thoughts to himself, she said as one might speak out of sleep: 'We had caught the sound of firing. We hadn't smelled the smoke yet but I guess we all knew that red flare in the south must be coming from Spanish 40. You couldn't see any stars in that direction at all. Archer's boys had just whirled, were starting to run for their horses, when Fenwick's bunch hit us.'

'Fenwick's bunch!'

'Certainly.' She looked up at him then and he could see the dark smudges the fire had left on her face. 'He was with them himself. I watched him boss the whole job.'

Price began to grasp the true measure of Flack's genius.

No brag, no bluster, no futile threats. The man had sat like a spider grimly biding his time until, plans readied and resources integrated, in one fell swoop he had brought down his wrath like a bolt from the blue, demolishing resistance, sweeping everything before it.

Look how cleverly he'd drawn Price away by the simple expedient of planting a suspicious horse on him and then, when the time was ripe, having Sparks use it for his dash into town. Every step of Flack's strategy had been carefully thought out and it was through no fault of his that Price had managed to escape; he had put enough men on the job in all conscience. He'd thrown Gill's Anvil crew at Archer and Fenwick's crew had put the bite on Sloan, not molesting the girl but stripping her of everything with which she'd thought to fight him.

Price slapped the stallion's neck and sighed. He had warned her what to expect of this business.

'I guess,' he said, 'you'll be pulling out now.'

'Pulling out for where?'

'Well . . . wherever you come from. Not much point sticking around any longer. You're licked and—'

'Licked?' she cried angrily. 'I haven't even begun!'

'Well,' Price growled, 'you've sure picked a heck of a time to start in. What you going to fight them with now, your bare hands?'

'I've still got this grass! And as long as I've got one cow to put on it—'

'You don't suppose, by God, he's passed up

113

them cattle, do you?'

She came onto her feet with a look hard as granite. 'Tuck your tail if you want to but *I'll* never quit!'

Price said, 'Look at this reasonable—'

'You're a fine one to talk! Instead of crying calamity at every turn why don't you work up a little ginger and take some pride in your outfit? We're a long way from licked! Nothing that really matters has been changed in the slightest—we're still alive, we're still here and we still own this grass. Pretty soon we'll have cattle on it—'

'Okay,' Price said, 'but what about your lumber?'

'We can get along without that—'

'Can you get along without Archer?'

She tossed off Joe Archer like a coat she'd grown out of. 'We've still got everything we had when we arrived here.'

Price let it ride. 'All right,' he said. 'You got us sittin' here cozy as two pups in a basket. What do you figure we had ought to do next?'

'Fire Fenwick's.'

So completely assured, so utterly and outrageously taken for granted, was her manner of delivering this preposterous statement Price's expression didn't change for perhaps as much as ten seconds. Then his face began to lengthen. The full shock of it hit him and it looked as though his eyes were about to roll off his cheekbones.

'Fire Fenwick's!'

'And what do you find so distasteful about that? I should think you'd want to get back at him. The man came over here, unprovoked, and destroyed everything he could lay his hands to. A dose of his own medicine should be just what that fellow is needing. If he thinks he can run roughshod over me he's got another think coming and I mean for him to know it!'

'Two wrongs don't make a right—'

Joyce sniffed. 'It's time these sidewinders learned to respect property and sitting here twiddling our thumbs won't help matters. We've got to strike while the iron's hot. I want you to—'

'You're out of your mind!' Price glared at her, flabbergasted. 'That jasper's got a crew of at least twelve men and when they passed around the salt that bunch was right at the head of the line. For the love of Pete, Sloan, let's be a little practical—'

'Very well,' she said scathingly, hands fisted on hips. 'If you're afraid to go over there I'll do it myself. But I should think, for what I'm paying you—'

'All right—all right,' Price grumbled. 'I'll see what I can do, but first I've got to get some sleep. You got anything around I can anchor this horse with?'

'That isn't the horse you borrowed from Shorty. What did you do—steal it?'

Price looked pained. 'As a matter of plain

fact, I had my legs spraddled out on the top of a gate when this bronc come along and took a run through 'em. Wasn't nothing I could do except to try and stay aboard him. Now if you've got any rope around—'

'I haven't even got a hairpin.'

'Well,' Price said, pulling off his belt, 'see if you can get this strapped around his front legs while I hold him. I would sure as hell hate to have to hoof it over to Fenwick's.'

They managed to get the horse hobbled and Price looked him over for bullet holes. He'd been creased on the hip in two places and there was that gash along his ribs where he'd smashed into the fence corner but none of these abrasions were anything to get up a sweat about. The sweat would come when Price tried to get back on him. For the moment, at least, he was docile and Price was too weary to think any further.

He went off in some bushes and dropped into the sand.

*　　　*　　　*

The sun was well down in the west when he came out of it and Sloan had evidently tried to fix herself up some. The smudges were scrubbed off her face and she gave him a friendly smile as he limped past, heading for the lake to scrub himself off a little.

He ached in every joint and had a taste in

116

his mouth like someone had boiled socks in it, but he felt considerably better after absorbing his share of river water. He shook out his clothes and, after he'd got into them, reckoned he would feel almost human again if he could stumble onto a razor and hack off some of these bristles.

He finally got out his knife, honed it on the sole of a boot and did what he could to make himself look presentable. But he sure wasn't looking forward to those next few hours of work she'd laid out for him. When it came to dealing with petticoats there was a lot to be said for the Indians, he reckoned.

The bronc was still around, still grazing and switching the flies off its scratches, and was a better looking hide than Price had last night imagined. Well set up, it showed the lines of good breeding and, shucked of its clowning, would make someone a staunch mount.

While he was still considering it Joyce came over with a couple of peculiar looking black things she held in greasy fingers.

'Rabbit,' she said. 'I borrowed your pistol, this morning and shot it.' When he didn't look too enthusiastic, she said: 'I know it isn't much, and I've got it a little more done than I'd intended, but it will help hold the wolf away. Which do you want, the back or this leg?'

'You eat it,' Price said—'you're probably hungrier than I am.' And then, with narrowing eyes going over her shoulder, 'Looks like we're about to get paid another visit.'

She turned and looked, standing so close he could smell the scrubbed cleanness of her. He felt an irritating impulse and killed it, and she said, 'Can you make any of them out?'

Price studied the bunch of loose saddle stock approaching and observed it was using the trail which came up from Spanish 40. He swiveled a chilling glance across the riders who came after them and allowed they were the three Archer'd fetched up here yesterday. Joyce didn't appear to like the tone or the look of him. She handed it down as her opinion Bar O was in no shape to be turning away help; and Price said, snorting, 'Those fellers couldn't help a blind fiddler into hell!'

'At least they've been thoughtful enough to bring horses—'

'Archer's whole cavvy by the looks . . . and you're right about that "thoughtful" part. There's a wagon coming back of them. Only thing they ain't fetched is the cattle, and I reckon—'

'I don't want you having any words with them. Or giving any cause for them to think we're not grateful.'

She said with her chin up: 'Do you hear?'

'He's seizin' this burn-out for a chance to move in on you. Let him bring in those horses and the next thing you know he'll be fetching in his cattle—'

'Never mind!' she said sharply. 'I shall tell

him he can if he wants to. How many others could you find in this country who would stake their whole future throwing in with a girl who is up against fellows like Flack. and Fenwick? Not many, I'll warrant. It's a really magnificent thing Joe is doing and I'll not have you acting like a dog in the manger—is that clear?'

Price growled in his throat. 'At least don't tell him where I'm off to tonight if you want me to get back.' But she was already hastening forward to greet them and he scowled at her lithesome back disgustedly.

Price hadn't any intention of swapping words with Archer but, because he hadn't any gear and foresaw the need of some on this job, he held up his departure till they'd got the horse stock headdown in the waving grass along an edge of lakefront. Then he beckoned the nearest rider. 'What's the chances of borrowing your rope for a minute?'

Shorty peered at him doubtfully. 'Where's that jughead I loaned you yesterday?'

'Another casualty to Flack.'

Shorty, reluctantly, pitched him his rope and abruptly his eyes, as they followed Price's movements, got big around as saucers. He came reining up behind him as Price dabbed a loop around the neck of the bronc which promptly went up on its hind legs, squealing. But Price, reaching a pass of the hemp around his buttocks, laid back on it, fetching the snorting stallion to ground.

Shorty, eyeing the belt which held its front legs hobbled, lifted a disbelieving glance at Price's waist and suddenly swore. 'Great balls of fire!' he gasped. 'Where in thunderation did you git that strawberry roan?'

'Copper State Feed & Livery. Sunflower,' Price said, not taking his eyes off the horse.

'Mean to say that dimwit let you *hev* him?'

'If you're referring to the proprietor, we didn't discuss the matter—'

'I should guess you didn't! An' you better not try t' git onto that devil—'

'How do you suppose I got him out here?'

'It's a cinch you never *rode* him,' Shorty snorted. 'That hide's throwed some of the slickest damn riders that ever blowed a stirrup between Santone an' Calgary! Only reason Flack's been keepin' him is for the pleasure of takin' falls outa wise guys like you. He's taken a fortune outa—'

'How about loaning me that saddle?'

With a sour grin Shorty came to earth, yanked the twist from his trunk strap, pulled it through the cinch ring and said, 'Where you want it?'

'Just up-end it there and drop the blanket across it hair side out. Then get back where you won't cramp this gentleman's style.'

'Ain't nothin' goin' t' cramp *his* style,' Shorty guffawed.

'Nor you ain't a goin' t' git that tree astride his back with out plenty help. An' I mean *good*

120

help!'

Price paid no attention to him but, waiting until the puncher had led his own still-bridled mount off, spoke quietly to the bronc and, bending, slipped the belt off its forelegs. Shorty's eyes looked like he was pretty well satisfied hell wasn't far from getting a chunk shoved under it.

Taking a short hold on the throw rope and twisting the slack of it around like a halter, Price coiling up the balance led the eye-rolling bronc over beside Shorty's saddle.

Catching hold of the blanket he let the horse smell of it, then tossed it across that red-and-white haired back. The stallion shivered, looked at Price, and softly blew through his nostrils. Price again spoke to him quietly and picked up the saddle. The animal laid its ears back and Shorty's bugged-out eyes began to shine with expectancy.

Price, continuing his meaningless monologue, left hand still wrapped about the shank of his improvised halter, held the saddle out by the horn with his right hand. The bronc danced away as far as the rope would let him, then twisted his head around as Price, clearing the skirts, settled the saddle on the blanket and, bending, caught the cinch and brought it up across his belly.

'What's the name of this bunch of dynamite?'

'You kiddin'?'

121

'Thought,' Price allowed, 'I might hang on longer if I had some kind of a handle.'

'You wantin' the crocheted article or one with brass rivets?'

Price grinned good-naturedly, bumped the horse in the wind and threw his weight on the latigo. Wedding Ring and Lippy had joined Shorty now and, over by the place where Fenwick had bonfired her lumber, Joyce and young Archer had turned their heads and were watching.

'If you call that dude "Snake" you won't be short-changin' no one,' Lippy told Price as the latter tucked the strap in.

Price shook the horn out of habit, then he led the big roan around a short circle, adjusted the stirrups and, very briefly, considered him. 'He ain't like,' Shorty said, 'to git no better with age.'

Price drew the horse's head around and put some weight in the stirrup. Watching the animal's ears he brought up his right leg and, when still nothing happened, fetched it over his back and settled his seat on the leather.

'My Gawd, is that *Snake*?' Wedding Ring cried, astounded.

'Good ol' Snake,' Price said, grinning at the look of them and slapping the horse affectionately. It was worth a month's pay, he thought, just to see their faces.

The bronc loosed a lugubrious sigh and then, while Price was still grinning, left the ground like a rocket, hind feet exploding where a moment ago his head had been. Price's left boot lost its stirrup. His seat came out of leather and the whole upper half of him was precariously canted above the reeling ground to the right of it when Snake buried his foretop and fished for the sun.

Price went down that bowed neck like a coon coming out of a tree in a hailstorm. But just as the ground looked about to tie into him those hind hoofs struck dirt like a wagonload of rock and that upswinging head flung Price back in the saddle.

He reckoned his top ribs must be rammed through his back. There was blood in his mouth and a whistling as of wind tearing across a greasewood flat came out of the roaring red fog where his eyes had been lost. But the coiled up end of that improvised halter was still cramped in the grip of Price's closed left fist and he drove in his spurs.

The horse lunged ahead with a bone-wrenching jerk, but though he still rode him blind Price had hold of him now and there was nothing the big roan could do but make tracks.

CHAPTER ELEVEN

Price, riding stiffly and trying all he could to favor his many bruises, came in sight of

Fenwick's ranch headquarters at what he judged to be about ten by the clock.

He hadn't rushed none to get here, knowing cowpuncher habits, and had taken plenty of time to get the roan enough in hand to where he figured he could put a little trust in its abilities. If they had to run for it he wasn't minded to be retarded by further demonstrations of his talent with pitching horses.

This was a serious business and could be right deadly if anything went wrong and he got trapped on these premises. He wasn't unduly put off his feed by the ethics of what Joyce had sent him here to do. This country hadn't been settled by chicken hearts and any man in Sloan's position, given the requisite amount of intestinal fortitude, would probably have looked at things pretty much as she had. What Price couldn't get himself reconciled to was finding that attitude in a woman.

He had been brought up in a God-fearing family which had ascribed definite limits to what a girl might do with impunity. The wearing of pants was a man's prerogative.

Price in many ways, while a product of his time, was considerably advanced in his thinking and was not inclined to hold the pants too much against her. But in his view—and his experience also—there were just two kinds of women in this world; and he was downright embarrassed to put the tag on Joyce Darling.

But how was a man to get around it? How else explain the rocky look of her stare when events or people didn't shape to her liking? And where had she got hold of all this cash she'd been spending?—her, a lone orphan!

Reluctant as he had been and still was to face the truth of it, he had finally got to the point where he could no longer shrug these questions aside. There'd been the way she had handled that guy on the stage . . . the tactics she'd employed to twist that fool of an Archer—and those tight shirts she wore! She knew too much about men. She was a girl with a past!

*　　　*　　　*

He peered ahead at that huddle of tarpaper-roofed buildings darkly standing like boxes against the night's patterned shadows, recalling this place as he had seen it last year. The big barn, the rambling ranch house, the saddle shed and smithy, the long and narrow bunkhouse; and the man whose industry and ruthlessness had built them.

He carried a pretty good picture of Fentwick in his mind; and had good cause to, he thought grimly, remembering again the parting words the man had flung after him. Although habitually clad after the manner of a cowhand in shield-fronted shirts and flaring bullhide chaps, no one would ever mistake

Bryce Fenwick for anything short of a tight-fisted owner. He had black gimlet eyes above a hawk's beaked nose and a cold-jawed look that would have soured fresh cream. He was a power in this country and he liked folks to know it. He wasn't going to like what Price had come here to do.

There was a grove of box elder just this side of the corrals which lay between these trees and the side of the harness shed. The bunkhouse flanked the shed but was off to the right of it with the barn behind it and the house beyond that. If he wasn't able to fire more than one of these buildings it would probably hurt Fenwick more to have his house go than anything. It was the showplace of the country.

It might be a little tricky though ducking past that bunkhouse to reach it, which he was going to have to do unless he rode this horse plumb around the place. He didn't much cotton to the idea of that; a critter like this Snake was a heap too unreliable to be used in any deal which could be played out without him; and he wanted him where he could get away quick, which he couldn't if he had to fetch him back around those buildings.

There were no lights showing, and he had counted on this likelihood in timing his arrival. Tying the horse securely in the blackest part of the box elder grove, Price made his way through the uncertain gloom until the planks

126

of the nearer corral loomed up before him. There were no horses in it.

Thrusting a leg between bars he moved into the pen and quietly crossed its circumference without untoward occurrence. He was both surprised and a little perturbed to find but three horses in the next one, for this was the corral commonly used by the crew for their saddle stock and there were no pens beyond it.

Some men faced with Price's mission might have rejoiced in this knowledge, but Price was a man who liked to see each step of the way before taking it and the unexpected absence of the crew opened up several ugly avenues of thought.

Considering these, he went down the line of planks separating the pen he'd just crossed from the occupied one and climbed out. One of the horses softly whickered and followed him around the side of the other as he approached with some stealth the nearest wall of the bunkhouse. He put an ear against the sheeting and caught the muted sound of snoring. One man probably, though it was possible there were two. Two out of the twelve he had expected would be in there.

Frowning, he crossed the yard, hearing snoring again as he passed the open door of the cook shack. Still hugging the deeper patches of gloom he went into the barn and broke three bales of hay open, scattering two of them about where they should do the most good. He scratched a couple matches looking around to make sure the place held no penned livestock, then dropped one into the scuffed-up hay, taking the bulk of the third bale with him as he slipped across to the house's back door.

It was not, of course, locked; and he doubted if there were anyone in it but, although he moved swiftly, he kept his eyes peeled on the assumption it was better to be sure than to wish you had. Fenwick was a bachelor but on account of his reputation Price went through all the bedrooms before he started piling up the livingroom furniture. He fired the rest of his hay and, leaving the front door open to insure a draft, stepped across to the cook shack. Jerking the dough-wrangler out of his blankets he left the man snarling profanity and struck out, still with his gun sheathed, for the bunkhouse.

All its windows were open but whoever had been making the high whine he'd heard through the back wall's sheeting had shoved the door shut, probably to keep out snakes.

Price, throwing it wide, discovered there were two of them; each was flat on his back with no other covering than the longhandled drawers he had sewn himself into.

'Fire! Fire!' Price yelled, and tossed a scratched match into the nearest heap of blankets. One of the erstwhile snorers, poking head above his chest, saw flame, smelled smoke and hit the floor swearing as Price ducked out.

Thirty feet of roaring flame enveloped the front of Fenwick's barn and smoke was funneling from its roof in great ballooning clouds. Swirling tatters of these drifted over the yard and clung like mistletoe in the cottonwoods' leafy branches; and wide patches of the yard were bright as day from the flames which, by now, were also bursting from the middle windows of the house.

Unlike Nero, Price had scant time for fiddling. As he rounded the end of the bunkhouse the cook opened up with a gun from the harness shed. Driven back around the corner Price cracked head-on into one of the pair routed out of the bunkhouse. Price saw the man's hand streaking beltward and slugged him. But the interval had given the fellow's compadre time to get into it. He made a stiff and enormous shape against the dancing light of the crackling flames and the upswinging gun blew two blasts from its barrel and the echoes of those shots smashed flatly against the sides of these buildings and hammered the night with their definite warning. One slug flung dirt and grit against Price's boots, the other withering past him with an outraged snarl; and he knew it was time to make the run for his horse.

He drew his gun but didn't use it. Instead, not wanting to spill blood if he could avoid it, he lunged back around the corner, hoping the *cocinero* might be hunting another position.

No slugs ripped out of the harness shed's shadow and he was half way down the back side of the bunkhouse, running crouched to present as small a target as possible, when the cook's 'Pull up!' came out of the blackness.

But the fellow waited too long. Flame tore from his gun just as Price crashed into him. He felt the breath of that bullet and knocked the cook's hand away; and then he was clear with the planks of the corral making black slats before him. He heard the cook, scrambling up, cursing wildly behind him.

He yanked the bars from the gate of the corral holding the horses and ran on, striving to put its wood between himself and those howling blue whistlers that were again trying to find him. With a crash of falling timbers he heard the barn roof go, tossing flame and sparks high above its doomed walls. This flare caught Price partway down the second pen.

*　　　*　　　*

Joyce, disengaging her hand, pulled away from Archer's arm and stepped out into the fire light with an evasive laugh in place of the answer he'd been sure she would give him. 'I'll have to think about that,' she said when he followed her. 'I've only known you a couple of days and marriage, after all, is a pretty serious proposition. I wouldn't want to say yes and then be forced to tell you I'd changed my mind.'

'Don't you worry about that.' His bold glance swept her shape with a male's yeasty confidence. 'What you need here's a man—'

'It wouldn't be fair to you, Joe, to let yourself get any further tangled in my affairs. You must remember you were able to get along with these men until—'

'You needn't take no blame for what they done over to my place; they'd of got to that anyhow sooner or later. It's you I'm thinkin' about. You're the biggest thing that ever has happened to me, Joyce, and I ain't aimin—'

'But you've done so much for me already!'

'The loan of a few horses? A load of grub and some blankets?' Archer's eyes sought hers hotly. 'I'd do a sight more than that—'

'But you've got to do a little bit of thinking about yourself, Joe; about your future—'

'Nothin' scary about my future if I had you to share it with me.'

'Gratitude and love don't always take the same trail, Joe. You don't know anything about me.'

'I guess I know what I want.'

'Please, Joe, let's don't rush this. While I'm with you I feel one thing, but how can I know how I will feel when you're gone? It seems to me that we should be a great deal better acquainted before we seriously think of taking

131

a step that would bind us together for the rest of our lives.'

'Mexicans—'

'But I'm not Mexican, Joe. Let's be practical a moment. Have you considered what may happen to your cattle while half your crew is over here? When Flack and Fenwick discover—'

'I know that,' he said stubbornly, 'but I ain't leavin' you to face them wolves by yourself.'

He scowled irritably into the shadows. 'The smart thing, of course,' he said as though it had just occurred to him, 'would be for us to throw our outfits together; consolidate the whole works right here in this Basin. That way, with my cattle moved over—'

'You can move them over any time you want, Joe.'

'Well . . . I dunno if your range boss would like that. He might get the wrong idea.'

'I think,' Joyce said, 'he's bright enough to see the advantages—'

'More to it than that. There's the matter of authority.'

'He would naturally be the boss,' Joyce said, 'so far as giving orders to the men would be concerned. It looks to me like a good idea. There are only three ways to get into this Basin and with that many guns we should be able to stand off the two F's indefinitely. If we could get the grub and enough ammunition.'

'No trouble about that. I brought this load

in from Bonita. While the boys are rounding up my steers I could fetch in some more. No, the way I see it, Price is liable to get his back up and kick over the traces. Probably tell you I'm movin' in to take this place from you. I think you ought to tell him straight off the way we feel about each other.'

Joyce said with calm assurance, 'Price will do what I tell him.'

Archer thought about that. 'I ain't noticed him around since he rode off on that horse. What's he doin' now?'

'He rode over to pay a little call on Bryce Fenwick.'

'On Fenwick!' Archer said, and his eyes narrowed down. 'Why didn't you tell me your crew had got in?'

'My crew hasn't got in. Price went over there alone.'

'Then I don't guess we need to fret our minds about him.'

'Of course not,' Joyce agreed. 'I don't hire the kind of men who require other men to look after them. Price will do what he went there to do then come back.'

Archer considered her through a tightening silence. 'And what was that?'

'He went over there,' Joyce said, 'to make Fenwick's place look like this one.'

CHAPTER TWELVE

Price twisted his head and in that gush of flame catapulting skyward from the collapsed barn roof saw the face of the cook forty feet behind him warping into an expression of savage satisfaction. The man had braked to a stop and was sighting down the barrel of a .47 caliber 'Paterson' Colt.

There was nothing Price could do but drop and fire, and he did both in a synchronous reflex smooth and deadly as the swoop of a hawk. He saw the cook's arms jerk—caught the glint of his teeth; and then Price was diving between planks, rolling across the pulverized manure and deep dust of the churned ground inside the pen, was coming onto his knees through a racket of slugs hammering into that fence and was running, doubled over, trying to make the far side and the black trees beyond.

He didn't quite make it.

He was the length of a horse from the creosoted timbers when the rails shook out a rattling from the thump of unseen lead. The crack-crack-crack of that high-powered rifle was a sound Price remembered with an impotent fury from the morning he and Joyce had ridden onto that bench below the Thief River crossing.

He went down on his belly and lay stiff as a

134

gopher till he counted the last crashing shot from the magazine; then, bounding to his feet, he made a lunge for the fence, paying no heed at all to the cork-stopped popping of the pistol coming at him from beyond the bronc pen planks. One slug cuffed his hat. Another jerked at his vest. But he got through the rails and was coiling into a crouch intended to hurl his aching muscle into a dash for the trees when a solid rank of horsemen came head-on out of their cover.

*   *   *

Sunny Cope, the round-bellied trail boss in charge of Bar O's herd of short-horned whitefaced cattle, was the picture of a cowman from his bootheels up. He had that hardtwisted look, was scarlet-cheeked and amiable as a bartender passing the time of day with a sheriff. More than one Texas tinbadge would have been exceeding glad for the chance of a word with him but the recipe for that read like the one for fixing bunny—i.e., first catch your rabbit.

He'd fetched only four hands to this cow-moving chore.

These were bleach-eyed men who looked to have been hired for reasons other than the talent they displayed in handling cattle. Cope ate with them and wiped on the same towel and so had not been much perturbed when, a couple of hours back, ten rifle-packing riders had come pell-mell out of the gathering dusk in an obvious attempt to stampede the bedded herd.

A good cowman's first thought would have been protection of his cattle but Cope, though he'd moved cows aplenty, was no cowman. He'd had his eyes skinned for trouble for the last fifty miles and, having pushed this bunch until there wasn't much run left in them, was as ready for it now as though he'd planned this raid himself.

He let the cows go and his crew along with them and put his whole attention to the job of emptying saddles. He didn't empty all of them but proved sufficiently proficient that inside of fifteen minutes there was no one left to shoot at.

When he caught up with the run-out herd he was no more bothered about the men he had killed than his crew would have been at finding worms in their biscuits.

'You wanta bed 'em down here,' a man called, 'or shove on?'

Cope pushed back his hat for a look at the stars.

'Ain't much more'n twelve mile to the home place, way I figure it. Might as well keep them movin' while they're easy to manage.'

'Knock a lot of weight off 'em.'

'They can pick up some more when they wade into that grass. Our job's to get them there—nothin' said about how.'

*   *   *

Price knew when he saw those riders coming at him there was nothing he could do but hold his ground and face it. To duck back through the rails would put him square in the sights of that fellow with the rifle. Better to stay where he was partially screened by the flame-swirled shadows thrown across him by the fence.

But his hope to go unnoticed was proved futile in mighty short order when a slug smacked into the upright behind him. Hope, he reflected, was for suckers, sugar coating the unpalatable facts of living with the mirage of a better tomorrow. It was like the things you could see looking into Sloan's eyes—a come-on for fools who hadn't ever grown up.

No use kidding himself about this deal. The flare from the barn was a dying roan stain hardly stronger than the shadows it still sought to disperse. But the fire in Fenwick's house was luridly coloring the yard; not bright enough yet that he could recognize faces but amply sufficient that he could find no break in that wave of advancing riders. They were coming four abreast, driving in for the kill.

Knowing he had reached the bitter end of all his dreaming, Price came up on one knee and tiredly lifted his pistol. Perhaps it was right that this fire he had kindled should prove the

137

means of his undoing. But there was in him a kind of sadness, a dismal feeling of regret that now he would never unravel the enigma of Joyce Darling, never learn the truth about her, never know what devils drove her or find the hateful answer to her sharp knowledge of men's ways.

He had his hunches and disliked them and, knowing he'd have no chance to reload, held his fire till the burliest shape in that pack rushing toward him loomed plain in his sights. He blinked the sweat from his eyes and, with the last of his thinking going down a black spiral, squeezed the trigger.

The dark shapes came on, their solidarity unbroken. He squeezed the trigger three times before he remembered Joyce saying she'd used his gun to get that rabbit.

*   *   *

Archer, after Joyce had dismissed him and gone off with her blankets, was irascible and restless. He hadn't the least doubt but that, given time, he could win her; but time looked like something he was about to run out of. She leaned too heavy on that range boss, and if he didn't get her promise before the crew showed up with those cattle she might take hold of the notion she could get along without him.

He wasn't the sort of man to stand for being held off and kept dangling. He knew he was attractive to women and believed the only thing that kept her backing and filling was the trust she put in that fellow Price and the chance the man held out to her for hanging onto this grass in her own right. Once get that whippoorwill out of the way and he reckoned she'd come to heel in a hurry.

He pulled up in a sweat of frustrated impatience and threw a black scowl at the black night around him. Some swift calculations narrowed the glint of his eyes and he stood still a moment, irresolute, while impulse and caution swung his thoughts back and forth to baleful gusts of greed and temper.

It wasn't in his mind any man could accomplish the thing Price had gone to Fenwick's to do, but if Price pulled it off and got back in one piece no one had to tell Archer he'd be done in this country.

He lifted muddy brown eyes and took a look toward his remuda. He rubbed his palms on his pantslegs. If he could snatch Price's defeat and turn it into victory, if he could successfully do the job Morg Price had got rubbed out attempting, it might be just the thing he needed to swing that girl in line.

He pushed it around a little longer, uneasily balancing the risk against the prospect of possible benefit. He had no intention of getting himself killed; thus, even though he failed as Price himself must do, he could fix it so she'd know he'd tried and, lacking Price to fall back on . . .

He checked it backward and forward, finally spreading his lips in a sly little grin. He got a cigar from his pocket and bit off the end and, going back to the fire, held a glowing stick to it. She would turn to him all right. In full earnest this time.

He dropped the stick back into the coals and tramped off through the dark where his men held the saddle band. Three minutes later all four of them were mounted and edging nervously away along the up-valley trail.

When they got beyond hearing Archer lifted his spotted gelding into a ground-eating gallop. Some forty-odd minutes later they dropped into the rocks of the river's old bed; following it south around the flank of the mesa. They were crossing the mouth of Shaketree Canyon when Archer, seeing light in the western sky, settled deeper into the saddle and fed his horse the steel.

They picked up the sound of gunfire. 'Got him trapped,' Shorty muttered; and Archer nodded, pleased. This was going to work out a lot better than he'd figured. No need to take any risk at all now.

He pulled down the showy gelding's pace a little, the others following suit. Price had fired the buildings, which was what they'd all come for, and Archer was almost persuaded to let it go at that until he realized he couldn't afford to. 'We'll slip into that grove of box elders,' he said, 'and try to get a line on what's happening.'

They drifted into the trees. 'There's his bronc,' Lippy grunted.

Archer nodded and pushed on, wondering what these fellows would think if he told one of them to loose it. Although strongly tempted he resisted the impulse, knowing there must be some smarter way which, if others later got onto it, could not be made to look so despicable.

He was presently able to assess the damage and convince himself Price was a bungler. The house was bound to go, the barn was just about finished and the bunkhouse had been leveled to a bed of glowing ashes but the harness shed, the cook shack and the corrals were still untouched. Furthermore, although he'd obviously loosed the saddle stock and so precluded any chance of pursuit, he'd been too slow to cut his stick and now was trapped by the light of his handiwork inside the larger of the pens—the one which lay closest to these trees.

Archer, peering through a pattern of interlaced branches, was endeavoring to place Fenwick's crew when he saw the perfect answer. One of the Turkey Track punchers was keeping Price jumping with the blasts from a high-powered rifle while another, with a belt gun, was sprinting down the corral's far side, angling toward that selfsame corner for which

Price himself was now ducking and dodging. Archer couldn't seem to spot the rest of Fenwick's bunch but suspected these were probably closing in through the shadows, holding their fire till they could get a sure shot.

The answer to his problems appeared engagingly simple. No call for sweat or bother; just let nature take its course.

Wedding Ring said from the corner of his mouth, 'If we're goin' to save that feller's bacon we had better be gettin' at it.'

Archer's glance caught the other two lifting their rifles.

'Let's hang and rattle a minute. He's all right for the moment. Before we go pokin' our snouts into this we ought to find out where the rest of that crew's at. We don't want them slipping up behind—'

'You want that guy to get shot into dollrags?'

Archer didn't care for the tone of Shorty's voice but kept a hitch on his temper and said with heavy patience, 'Of course I don't want him shot into dollrags, but I don't want you boys carried off on shutters, either. Won't hurt to stay here long enough to find out where they're at.'

They watched Price reach the fence and come through it, dropping onto the ground where the light was poorer. The man working the .45–90 was still now and Price came onto one knee, lifting his pistol and looking toward the pen's corner. 'He knows,' Archer murmured, 'where that ranny's goin' to show. You don't need to worry about that fellow—'

'Listen!' growled Wedding Ring harshly, half turning; and Archer threw an apprehensive look across his shoulder. They all caught it then, the rushing pound of shod hoofs pulsing out of the blackness, now lifting, now falling, but steadily drawing nearer.

'Py damn,' Lippy grunted, shifting uneasily in his saddle—'who you think iss coming, eh?'

'No friends of ours, that's sure,' Shorty muttered; and Wedding Ring said, 'We better get out of here.'

The man who'd been stalking Price to the fence corner hadn't yet rounded it. Price himself had turned and was eyeing the trees when a thought clicked over in Archer's mind and he knew just as sure as he knew his own name it was the rest of Fenwick's crew closing in.

For one frozen second the knowledge clamped his nerves in a paralysis of fright. Then he cursed and went spurring out into the open, the other three with him, trying to hurl himself across that firelit yard and get behind the shelter of cook shack or harness shed before Fenwick's riders got him lined in their sights.

He saw Price come erect and threw a shot at him. Shorty stiffened and pitched wordlessly out of his saddle. Lippy, triggering frantically,

143

knocked the man over who rushed out from the fence corner.

They rounded it into the full glare of the flames and the rifle took up its crack-cracking again and the air hummed with pellets as a volley crashed out of the blackness behind them. One strangled yell tore from Lippy's stretched mouth and beside him Wedding Ring, riding Indian fashion, fetched his free hand around and emptied his pistol.

Archer, careening into the swirl of shadows back of the cook shack, fumbled fresh loads into the mechanism of his gun, dropped it into its leather and dragged the rifle from beneath his left knee. Wedding Ring, still astride the snort and pitch of his now spooked pony, vanished around the harness shed's corner and shortly his gun was kicking fresh bursts of sound into the muted uproar of squealing horses and cursing men.

Archer reined his own mount into the deeper gloom of a mesquite tree and swung his rifle duck hunter fashion across the short arc between the two one-room buildings, waiting for something to ride into his sights. He saw Wedding Ring, gun emptied and with nothing exposed but one knee and an elbow, go tearing off north into the thickening curdle beyond the reach of the flames. Three Turkey Track punchers in full cry spurred after him.

One part of a promise drifted out of their wake as they drove past Archer's ferny thorn-laced cover. Clear and distinct—it was Fenwick's voice—heard even above the slashing pound of those hoofs, through wind, shout and gunfire: '—two hundred dollars for the man who drops Archer!'

It was spark to the tow of the hidden man's turbulence and he jerked up his rifle, muzzle light showing the wicked shape of his fury as he flung his slugs after them. Fenwick, spun half around on his mount by the impact, threw up both hands and slid off his horse backwards. The man to his right swayed and clutched for the horn but the third raced off unscathed into blackness.

CHAPTER THIRTEEN

It was getting on for daylight with the leaden reef of clouds behind the soot-colored crags of the eastern mountains showing cracks of cerise and magenta when Price, tiredly forking a Turkey Track cow horse, rode wearily into Joyce Darling's camp. It was getting, he thought, to be a kind of habit, coming home in the small hours to find Sloan alone.

'It's done,' he told her—'burned to the ground.'

'Did you see Joe Archer?'

He stared at her through the gloom for several pounding heartbeats, at last getting out of the saddle. 'Had a notion it was him. How'd he come to be over there?'

She didn't answer right away, and when she finally did there was an unaccustomed diffidence in her voice which surprised him. 'I thought,' she said hesitantly, 'you might need some help.'

'So you send that damn lapdog!'

The anger kindled by the thought came very near to getting away from him and he stood with locked fists and clamped lips till he mastered it, afterwards grunting, 'You got anything I can eat around here?'

She considered him a moment, started to put out a hand but turned away without speaking, moving across to a dark mound and lifting back the end of a piece of canvas laid over it. By the time he got the borrowed horse unsaddled and turned out with the bunch from Spanish 40's remuda she'd got a blaze above the coals and was frying eggs and bacon. Coffee's pungent smell hit the hollow of his stomach and he dropped onto a nearby rock and dozed with elbows on knees till she called him.

He was sipping his second cup of coffee when hoof sound brought his head around and he saw a rider coming toward them from the direction of the bench. He went on drinking, watching the man over the rim of his cup. Day was brightening in the east and he caught the cold glint of metal winking off the man's shirt before the fellow got near enough to make out his features. Price would have known it was Flack's brother even without the star.

He watched the man come up to their fire and sit there awhile staring down without speaking. He had a pair of slate eyes above an unruly facsimile of Flack's neat mustache and cheeks that were gray as the racked clouds above them.

'Your name Price?'

'It always has been.'

'When you left town the other night you went off on a nag that happens to be private property. Where is it?'

'I don't know.'

Flack's brother was too old a hand at this game to let an accused man take refuge behind ignorance. 'You better find out, and find out fast, if you don't want a horse-stealing charge slapped against you.'

Joyce was looking a little nervous but Price, cup in hand, was peering up at the marshal like he thought this business was some kind of gag.

'Think you'd know that horse if you saw him?'

'Certainly I'd know him.'

'Better take a prowl around then. If you locate him here—'

'I don't have to locate him. They're trying to give you a break, but if I can't pick up the horse I've got orders to fetch you in.'

Price looked into his cup, idly swirling the

147

coffee. With no warning at all he came onto his feet, flinging coffee and cup at the officer's face. When Flack's cursing brother got Price again into focus he found himself staring down the bore of a pistol.

'You're kind of off your reservation,' the tall cow boss was informing him—'a long ways off it. When you get back into your bailiwick you can tell that precious brother of yours that if he wants to go on breathing he better lay off this spread. Because, if he don't, I'm liable to come in after *him.*'

'Sorry about breaking that cup,' Price said to Joyce, still watching the marshal dwindling into the distance. 'I guess that fellow kind of got my goat.'

She picked up his plate and her own, then said impulsively, 'For a forty a month puncher you're pretty handy with that thing.'

Price, following her glance to his holster, said dryly, 'If it's all right with you, I'm going to catch a few winks.'

'Tell me first about Turkey Track—what happened over there? Why didn't Joe Archer come back with you?'

'Don't know,' Price said. 'Maybe he had other plans.'

'Well, what happened?'

'Several punchers got killed.' It was plain Price didn't like it but, under the girl's demanding look, he said gruffly, 'I fired the barn, the house, the men's sleeping quarters.

Archer killed Fenwick.'

His eyes narrowed then. He stepped away from the girl and Joyce, turning, saw a horseman approaching from the direction recently taken by the departing town marshal. It looked like Sparks.

It *was* Sparks.

He eased his horse to a stop a few feet away, and with his empty hands folded over the horn sat regarding them with a grin, at last saying, 'They did better in the Bible. Killed a fatted calf if you can believe what they tell you.'

'You'll get no fatted calf here,' Price said grimly.

'Still on the prod, eh?' He let his bright glance play over the girl, then brought his eyes back to Price again. 'I didn't look for much gratitude. When a man's knocked around.'

'You can skip all the platitudes.'

Amusement broadened Sparks' grin. 'No need to push on the reins. Thought when I was here before you seemed kinda partial to that nag I took off on. How much would you give to put your hands on the picture that come off his off hip?'

'So that's your game, is it?'

Sparks, lifting one eyebrow, hauled the makings from a pocket and proceeded to roll himself a smoke. 'No game about it. I'm a businessman, bucko; what I'm offerin' is a trade—your dough for my knowledge.' He flicked his tongue across the paper. 'That's fair enough, ain't it?'

Joyce asked Price, 'Do you know what he's talking about?'

'Taffy colored hide I bought from the livery.'

'But what's this business about a picture?'

'Horse gave me the notion he belonged on this place.'

Her green eyes, going wide, incomprehensibly searched his features. 'And you think he might be one of the old Bar O bunch?'

Price shrugged, his glance stony.

'But his brand was a turtle . . .'

Sparks' grin licked over his lips again. 'On the hair side it was.'

Joyce, ignoring him, continued to watch Price, and something she found in the look of him caused her to say with a sudden impatience, 'What difference can it make? I didn't buy any stock—'

'You bought the Bar O land and brand, didn't you? You want a club you can use on that gambler, don't you? All right then,' Sparks said, 'I've got one to sell an', just to show you my heart's in the right place, Missy, I'll chuck in a few words to go along with the patch I skun outa that pony.'

Joyce considered him doubtfully. 'How much would you want?'

'We ain't buyin',' Price said before the

businessman could answer.

Sparks grinned imperturbably. 'You don't wanta lose that herd, do you? I'll say this much for nothin': *Flack's found out where it's at.* Looks like five hundred cartwheels wouldn't be too stiff a drain to prove the guy's a rustler still workin' at his trade.'

Joyce, chewing her lip, wheeled away a few steps and came around with the tobacco tin Price had seen on the dresser in her room at the Orrison. She had the lid thrown back and was inserting rummaging fingers when Price reached out and stopped her. 'What do you expect to get out of a mouthful of lies?'

'Why don't you keep out of this!' Sparks snarled with a look of outrage. 'They're her cattle, ain't, they? Let'er make her own mind up!'

He took a couple of glowering moments to get his thoughts lined out again and then, with what he presumably supposed to be a reassuring smile, declared to the girl, 'It's true Flack sent me out here to find out all I could about you. An' mebbe,' he said gruffly with a hard scowl at Price, 'I don't stack too high by *some* people's figgerin', but I wasn't brought up to wool women an' kids. Only thing, you understand, it's a damn hard world an' I got to git mine. Just slip me five hundred so's I can git outa this country an' I'll give you enough on Flack to hang him higher'n a kite.'

Price said, advancing, 'I'll give you

151

something—' but Sparks yanked his horse back. With his boxer's face turned ugly he rasped, 'All right, Missy, I gave you the chance! When you start walkin' outa here with nothin' on your back but that la-de-dah shirt, you can thank this smart cooky—Hey! Watch yourself, damn it—leggo of my foot!'

'Let him go,' Joyce said and Price reluctantly turned Sparks' boot loose.

'You'll find it's cheaper in the long run to step on a centipede when you've got him handy.'

* * *

Price came awake to the bawl of milling cattle. Knuckling the sleep from his eyes he found them all around both shores of the lake and some were standing in it with the water clean up to their briskets. He thought, staring over the ground at them, they made a picture to gladden any rangeman's heart until, his glance abruptly lifting, he saw another herd approaching from the direction of the notch.

This second bunch, catching the damp smell of water, were doing their utmost to boil into a run and the gesticulating riders, trying to keep the herds from mixing, appeared to be having about all they could handle.

It was the color of this new bunch, suddenly registering, that pulled Price onto his feet with a curse. These were Herefords—Joyce's cattle!—which meant that bunch around the lake was probably stuff from Spanish 40.

Now, he thought, *maybe she'll believe what I tell her.*

Just the same he was jolted. He hadn't actually credited Archer with the guts to move in on her; his warning had been of a play he'd considered an uncomfortable possibility not too likely to materialize. But now the cattle were right here on the ground and, with dark coming down, if that herd got away from the Bar O crew—Hell's fire! There it went!

Price swore disgustedly.

Peering through the drift of dust he caught sight of Joyce beside a pulled-up wagon. Two men were on the seat and the nearest man was Archer. With his look turning bleak Price headed in their direction.

Coming in from the side farthest removed from the cattle he could see that the bed of the wagon was crammed to the guards with cases of tinned foods, sacked flour and sugar and what seemed to be a good many boxes of pistol and rifle cartridges. No man, Price decided, would go to so much bother without he was counting on staying for awhile.

He came up and stopped almost within reach of them without either man appearing to notice. Archer, what time he wasn't putting the hex on Joyce, was watching the two herds mingle with every evidence of inward satisfaction. The other fellow, an older, more hard-bitten replica of Joe, had a rug tucked around his legs and was sitting there stiff as parfleche-wrapped rock with his gnarled hands gripped about the shanks of a pair of crutches. No one, Price thought, considering the man, would ever pick this fellow for Santa Claus. Sharp bones jutted craglike above his sunken cheeks and the eyes glaring out of those rocketed hollows were fixed on the girl with a look of indescribable bitterness.

They had, apparently, just driven up for Joe was still talking with Joyce about his cows. 'Them two rannies that helped Weddin' Ring push 'em over have come down with cold feet and will be pullin' out shortly; but we'll make out to get along all right. We'll put all your hands to watchin' the passes—'

There was a fellow cutting over from the lake on a sorrel and Joe broke off to watch him, scowling as this waddy swung his mount in their direction. It was beginning to get dark but Joyce made him out. 'That's Sunny Cope,' she said, 'a gun fighter I hired in El Paso to trail my herd up. He can cut the buttons off your shirt at thirty paces with a pistol.'

Joe's head jerked around and he looked like a man who'd had a snake crawl up his pantsleg. Price's glance sharpened, too; and then Cope was with them; neckreining his grulla walkin-stick up on the shoreward side of old Wrapped Knees, poking his hat at the girl and saying, 'I sure didn't aim to let them herds

154

git mixed thataway—'

'It doesn't matter,' Joyce said. 'I want you to recognize Joe Archer who speaks for Spanish 40; that's him standing in the wagon.'

Joe, thus reminded of his manners, jerked Cope a nod and told the girl: 'This here's my father—'

Jelks Archer, leaning forward with a balked and intolerant anger blazing out of his bitter stare, pushed his words uncaringly through his son's talk to say directly to Joyce, 'So you've come back!'

CHAPTER FOURTEEN

Many things clicked into place for Morgan Price in that moment; almost forgotten unrelated details which, though building up a tension in him, had appeared to hold no real significance until touched by the alchemy of Archer's voice. Now confusion no longer blinded him, the pattern emerged with a metallic clarity and each seemingly loco move Joyce had made stood revealed in sharp focus with its burden of hate.

'Yes,' she said, 'I've come back, Mr. Archer.'

Price thought the smile she gave that old man was the hardest thing he had ever looked at. So deep went the bitter corroding malice of the determination which had driven and was driving her there was nothing left in the shape of her face to remind him of the girl he had met on the stage.

It was the face of a stranger, the face of the things she had stored in her head through all the years she had been gone from this Basin. It was twin, Price thought, for the look of Jelks Archer who now rasped disparagingly, 'Back to pay off the grudge of a drove out squatter!'

'Whatever the reason,' Joyce answered, 'I'm back. Get that wagon unloaded,' she cried harshly at Joe.

Joe, starting to turn, flung one confused look from the girl to his father. 'Have you two met before?'

Old Archer eyed his son with an unsparing glance. 'Don't make yourself out a bigger fool than you are. Get this team turned around and take me away from here.'

'Sunny,' Joyce said, 'keep that team where it's at until he empties this wagon.'

Wedding Ring came up and the old man grabbed at Joe's arm. 'Tell your crew to round up my cattle—'

'You're behind the times, Archer. You've no cattle here. Every cow on this grass belongs to Bar O.'

Young Archer looked at her, startled. 'B-but you told me—' he stammered; and she laughed in his face. Congested blood thrust its flush above the line of his collar, but he shook his head doggedly. 'You told me I could push our cows here!'

'You pushed them.'

'But you gave me to understand—'

'That old man sitting side of you gave my father to understand some things, too, that didn't turn out as he was led to believe they would. And you weren't above trying some of that stuff yourself. Sunny,' she said, coolly watching Joe's father, 'as soon as we get done with this I want the bulls cut out of that Spanish 40 herd and shot. Every last one of them—*do you hear*?'

'Yes, ma'am. It'll be took care of,' Cope said, grinning at the look of Joe Archer's face.

It was the old man Price was watching, and he shook his head, not liking this.

Joe didn't seem to care a lot for it, either. There was a storm rushing through him and some of its wildness got into the strangled yell that burst out of him. 'Weddin' Ring! Damn it, don't sit there like you been glued to that saddle! Put your gun on these bastards!'

The Spanish 40 hand gave Joe a hard stare, folded his fists across the horn and spat without answering.

Sweat gleamed beneath Joe Archer's hat rim and the angry remembrance of things past but not done with wrote their bitter reflections across his cheeks. He was like a coyote trapped in this circle of faces. He shook his shoulders together and eyes that revealed too much white round the pupils clawed their way through the hate to fasten bleakly on Joyce.

'Last night,' he growled hoarsely, 'I killed Bryce Fenwick for you. Don't that count for anything!'

Price saw the girl's lips curl. Saw Wedding Ring's glance turn away very bitter. And then Joe snarled in his outrage, 'I ain't forgettin' this, baby! No plow-chaser's brat's goin' to make a fool of me!'

The old man looked at Joe drearily. 'Don't make remarks you're going to have to crawl out of.'

'I ain't crawlin' out of nothin'!' Joe shouted. 'I'll make her rue this day if it's the last thing I do!' He burned a wicked glance around that circle of watching faces and was snatching up the lines and furiously reaching for the whipstock when Cope, easing his horse forward, said; 'Take it easy, kid. You ain't goin' noplace till you unload that wagon.'

*   *   *

After the Archers and their hands had pulled out, heading south, Joyce introduced Sunny Cope to Price. 'You'll be getting your orders from him,' she told Cope.

The gun fighter's opaque eyes looked Price over. He gave a noncommittal grunt. 'I'd suppposed,' he told the girl, 'when I got up here with them cattle, I'd be down on the payroll as right bower in this outfit. I'm a

158

natural born boss, if you get what I mean. Them boys may not cotton to workin' for this feller.'

'How is that?' Joyce asked.

'Well . . .' He looked at Price. 'You know the way these tough monkeys are.'

Price nodded soberly. He could see what Cope meant. And if this thing happened to get pushed to an issue there was nothing to prevent this gunhawk and his pals from riding away with every cow in this Basin. It was not a situation to be resolved by a show of force because the force, in this instance, would be all on Cope's side.

'I been hired as ranch manager,' Price said, feeling the ground out. 'I don't see any reason why you shouldn't have charge of the crew. I could write you down in the book as foreman. How would that strike you?'

Cope chewed it over, pulling his long nose thoughtfully. 'I expect that might do. So long as you don't git too free with the gab.'

'I suppose you know,' Price told Joyce, 'what Archer's bound to do now? He'll send the law in here after you for holding those cows.'

Cope winked at the girl. 'That scares us to beat hell.'

Joyce rested a hip against the mound of sacked flour. She glanced impatiently at Price. 'You've already run the law out of here once—'

'It won't be that kind of law,' Price said

grimly. 'Flack will call in the sheriff, or he will have Archer do it, and he will get all his leatherslappers sworn in as deputies. They'll come flapping out here like a congress of buzzards and if you thumb your nose at them—'

'Where'd you find this crepe-hanger?' Cope growled; and then, snorting, he told Price, 'If this Flack's got any wheels at all in his think-box he'll sure keep 'em spinnin' right smart of a while before he ties into us again. For your information, somebody made a pass at them whitefaces last night an' five of that outfit's still layin' where I dropped 'em. Flack ain't goin' to overlook no warnin' like that.'

'That was Fenwick's bunch,' Price said stubbornly.

'All right,' Joyce said, 'Fenwick's out of it. Archer drilled him and you fired his buildings. Whatever's left of his crew is probably long gone by this time.'

'An' it's a cinch Archer's busted,' Cope chucked in like he was Moses.

'Joe will tie up with Flack,' Price predicted. 'You heard him tell Sloan—'

'That guy tells a lot of things besides his beads. He was just blowin' off. His old man knows what the score is.'

'They would hardly turn to Flack,' Joyce decided, 'after the way that bunch from Anvil hit them,' and Cope, with a patronizing grin at Price, nodded.

'We don't need to worry no more about them.'

Sensing the futility of further argument Price buttoned his lip. But the thoughts kept spiralling around in his head and, after a bit of reflection, he presently asked Joyce, 'Don't you think it might still be a pretty good idea for us to put a few men to watching those trails?'

She, correctly gauging his mood, said, 'Of course,' and there was an interval of silence while she and the gun fighter traded looks. Then Cope, glancing testily at Price, wanted to know how many ways there were of getting in here.

'There's the river trail past Archer's, there's the one coming in from the north over the bench and there's the notch trail winding through the mountains out of Anvil.'

'Three,' Cope growled, ticking them off on his fingers, 'an' I got only four hands. That ain't leavin' much help to do the work of this outfit.'

'I guess you and me could manage to do it for awhile,' Price said, 'and we could use that other fellow for running errands and carrying orders.'

'I can see him runnin' errands. That "other feller" is the cook. You better not try tell *him* what to do.'

Price shrugged his shoulders. Joyce said to Cope, 'It's going to be dark pretty soon. You

161

better tell the boys to start killing those bulls. Have them dress a couple out—'

Price said, 'If Archer brings the sheriff in here—' and Cope, flinging his head around, snarled, 'Why'n't you write a song about it!'

'Just the same,' Price said, doggedly intent on making his point, 'those fellows will collect for every bull we slaughter—'

'They'll play hell, too! They can't make her pay for a golrammed thing! Her old man owned this Basin an' she's paid up the back taxes. She's got a cast-iron case against Archer for trespass—'

'The laws of trespass don't apply to open range without your place is properly fenced and in this state, amigo, that means five strands of wire. On top of damages—'

'We'll "damage" them all right if they come yowlin' around here! You think she wants them good whitefaced cows droppin' grade stuff by them damn scrub bulls? What the hell kinda manager are you, anyhow!'

And, with that parting shot, Cope rowelled his horse toward the lake, still breathing fire and brimstone.

Price, turning disgustedly to Joyce, asked gruffly, 'Does it still taste sweet to you?'

'I don't know what you're talking about.'

'This revenge you been thirsting for. Breaking that crippled old man up—'

'That "crippled old man",' Joyce blazed, with her chin up, 'played my Dad for a sucker

162

and any misery I can deal him won't be a patch to what he's got coming! He deliberately talked Dad into a string of bad investments that took every cent we had, and then he talked the bank into refusing to give us credit. We had a big hay crop coming on and just about the time it was ready to harvest, Fenwick came in with his range roughers and burned it. He ran a bunch of his cattle through our millo maize and ruined it. Then his men came in an' uprooted our orchard—'

'Archer's men?'

'No, Fenwick's; but they were all after Dad; and the owner of Anvil, too—he was in it. I understand he was killed a couple of years later, in some kind of a saloon brawl. Anyway, Flack got his outfit and took his place in the Combine.

'But my Dad had a lot of sand in his craw and, when they saw he was too bull stubborn to quit, Fenwick's crew came into this Basin one night and moved us out bodily. They took us halfway to Hayden and turned us loose on the desert without water, food or horses. Dad never got over it.'

Price stood silent and after a bit Joyce said, 'I don't think we need to worry overmuch about Flack & Company fetching the law into this; no outside law, certainly.'

Price thought Flack would probably now gobble Turkey Track—at least, make the attempt. For he would then, with Archer's spread as good as in his pocket, be in a position to inspect and regulate travel to and from the Basin. Since there was nothing to be gained by advising Joyce of this he did not mention it, but he was a long way from sharing her expressed conviction Flack would fail to use the law as a means for getting her out of here.

Why shouldn't Flack use it? Joyce hadn't a particle of evidence against him—nor had Price; although they might, if things got too uncomfortable, create a minor diversion by naming Flack the accomplice of murderers and charging young Archer with Fenwick's killing. But this, he thought, would be a dubious move so long as Bar O had Cope on its payroll. Better all around, he was forced to conclude, if the girl was proved right and Flack kept the law out of this.

The shadows were no longer individual shapes and the barking of pistols along the lakefront had stopped. A few cows were still bawling but the bulk of both herds, he judged, was beginning to bed down. Night was almost upon them. The silent cook, working back of his groaning cart, was crouched above his kettles and the voices of the crew occasionally drifted across the flat without decipherable meaning.

Miles above them a thin sprinkling of stars glimmered faintly and Joyce, against the mound of sacked flour, was an indistinct blackness below a pale blob of face whose expression he could not read.

A coyote's yammer lifted out of the deepening gloom. The strain of this job was sinking its barbs in Price and the shape of things to come, whenever he let his thinking touch Cope, increased his unease. A fed-up restlessness moved through him and the prodding of long hungers, again awakened by this girl's proximity, made him clench his fists behind him until the nails dug into his palms.

She must have felt his regard though she gave no sign of it.

'Hate,' he said, 'is a lot like a canker. A bad thing for anyone to hug too close, Sloan.'

Her head came around and his hand touched her shoulder and she seemed, trembling, to sway nearer. His grip tightened and felt the warmth of her and shock slammed wildly through him, tearing down the barriers; and he grabbed her, roughly swinging her against him. A high wind sang through him and she was a willow, rocked with motion. Her lips were against his fiercely. He felt the trembling go through her and then her hands were between them, fending him off, violently thrusting at him. She tore her mouth away. 'Please, Price! Don't—'

Thoroughly aroused he used his strength to fetch her back to him, used it uncaringly, trying again to recapture her lips. But her twisting face eluded him and finally, angrily, he dropped his arms and watched her back off breathing heavily.

He sleeved the sweat off his face and watched the sharp rise and fall of the breasts pressed so tight against the cloth of her shirtfront. And it was in his mind to get hold of her again but she thrust out an arm. 'It won't do, Price.'

'Why won't it?'

She shook her head at him. 'You don't know anything about me—'

'I guess, by God, I know when I want a woman!'

'That's just it. How *long* would you want me?'

'You think I go round making a practice of—'

'It isn't that. I told you how we quit this place. Where do you suppose I got the money to come back here again with these cattle and gun men?'

All his black suspicions came crowding back, filling his head with their ugly clamor; and she said, very low, as though the words were wrenched out of her, 'You would always be wondering . . .'

He wanted to say he didn't give a damn but the words stuck in his throat. He couldn't get them out, could only stare at her, bleakly, sick with the shame of it and cursing himself for the folly of inaction, in that moment almost hating her.

'You could tell me,' Price growled.

'But there would still be the wonder. I had to eat. I had to take care of Dad.' She sighed a little, sadly. 'Those are the things you'd be all the time wondering.'

'I guess I know what I want,' Price grumbled, but his tone lacked conviction and the both of them knew it.

An uncomfortable silence followed Price's words. Wanting desperately to break it he could find nothing to say. His sweat-dampened body became aware of the chill flowing down off the Rhinestones and his mind told him fall would soon be fleeing the breath of winter; and he hated himself, not for what he had done but for not going through with it.

And then her head swung sharply and his own was swinging with it and the sound of shod hoofs was drumming out of the north. One horse, coming fast off the trail from the bench.

He felt the girl suddenly pressed against him; and his left arm snaked out and swung her behind him, the spread fingers of his right slashing down to his gun.

A voice sang out in challenge from the direction of the nervous cattle, and the cook ducked away from the shine of his fire as the hoofs thundered toward it. Price broke into a run, Joyce running with him, and they got to the wagon just as the rider slid his horse to a stop.

He made a wild looking figure, hatless and

whiskered, with the light of the flames dancing back from his rifle. 'Uncle Jim!' the girl cried; and he said, 'Quick—where's your father?'

'Dad's gone. Is there anything I can do?'

'You better try. There's a hell's smear of horsemen coming down off the stage road!'

CHAPTER FIFTEEN

They were nearly to the burned-over site of the home place before Joe's old man opened his mouth. He looked ten years older than he had on the up-trip. Pulling the rug closer about his knees he asked bleakly, 'You got any idea what you're going to do now?'

Joe's surly look tightened.

'Because if you haven't we'll head for Safford and put our case before the sheriff.'

Joe Archer snorted. 'You don't think that puddin'head would stick his jaw out, do you?' He said as though his father should be given a string of spools, 'I got a better hunch than that. I'm goin' to see Ira Flack.'

'You'd crawl back to him? You got no more pride than that?'

'I ain't never seen no one puttin pride in a kettle—'

'Pride is the difference between a man and a dog.'

'I'll *be* a dog then, but I'll get back at that

slut if it's the last thing I do! Flack'll know how to handle that outfit.'

'He ain't had any considerable luck up to now.'

Joe looked at him blackly. 'Why the hell don't you stay one way or the other?'

'If you had enough sense to get out of a hailstorm we never would have come to this pass in the first place—'

'An' if I'd listened to you we'd been froze out long ago. This way, at least, we got somethin' to bargain with. It's been plain all along he meant that grass for himself. So we'll sell him Spanish 40; range, brand, cattle an' everything.'

'He ain't going to buy what he can grab off for nothing, and when it comes to the cattle we haven't got any to sell him.'

'I don't see how you got along before I come.' There was this intolerance in Joe, this top-lofty conceit that wouldn't compromise with patience. He was a man with no slack between desire and action. 'Pay them damn hands off and I'll show you how to cook two birds with one fire.'

The old man grunted but he called up the men. The pair who'd been going to quit anyway took their money and rode off through the curdled gloom of the pines. Wedding Ring said he'd just as lief string along.

'I don't want a man around,' Joe growled, 'that won't take my orders.'

'I'll take 'em quick enough when they make sense.'

'You're too particular. Pay him off,' Joe told his father. And when the man had reluctantly gone, Joe said, 'What's the thing Flack wants most in this country? That Basin grass, ain't it? All right, I'm going to show him how he can get it. Soon's he buys us out I'll give him that Basin on a platter.'

'How?'

'You seen the kinda hands that girl's hired? Bunch of damn gunslicks that'll fight at the drop of a hat an' no questions. Now when Flack buys us out he becomes legal owner of everything packin' the Spanish 40 brand— which means all of them cattle that slut's took away from us. By backdatin' the sale he can show as owner when she took 'em. So he goes to the sheriff, tells him about the fire at Fenwick's, tells him the girl has burned Spanish 40 an' drove off all these cattle. Then he swears out a warrant . . .'

'The sheriff ain't goin' to want nothin' to do with that kind of tough outfit. So what does Flack do? He gits Jack Gill, his ramrod at Anvil, made special deputy to take care of the business. When they git back to town Gill can swear in a bunch of them barflies an' range bums with just enough of his hands to make sure of the outcome. Bar O's goin' to fight, which is all the excuse Gill will need to rub the whole bunch out.'

'He can do all that without handing us a cent.'

'That's right,' Joe grinned thinly. 'But he won't know about the cattle until I tell him. An' I ain't tellin' him nothing until we've got the cash in hand.'

* * *

'Who's this feller you got with you?' The hatless rider peered at Price and then, apparently, forgot him. 'Your father ought to be told, girl.'

'Dad's gone on—he's dead,' Joyce answered, and the whiskered rider clucked with frank sympathy.

'Redskins! Allus knowed them devils would be the death of him. Too careless, Ed was. Too forbearin'. I told him—'

'Uncle Jim,' Joyce cut in, 'this is my cow boss, Morgan Price.'

'Cows!' the whiskered rider said testily. 'What you want to sink your all into them for? Country's plumb overrun with the dratted critters now. 'Pache bait, I calls 'em. Won't bring you in a dollar a penful. You ought to done like your Daddy an' stuck with the hay.'

'We had hard luck with our last crop. And this is our cook,' Joyce said, 'Slow Poison.'

The crochety rider pulled his hatless head around. A snapping branch in the fire sent up a brighter flare and Price noticed the thong now that, coming down through his whiskers, was passed under his jaw like a chin strap. He peered harder at the top of the fellow's head and got a damn peculiar feeling in the pit of his stomach. The old man's head was covered with dog hair.

'You've named him well, I'll say that for you. Never et after a ranch cook yet that—'

'And this is Morgan Price, my ramrod,' the girl repeated before the humped-up cook could get a hand on his meat axe.

The collie-haired old codger said, 'I been seein' him around;' and Price asked:

'You saw those fellows coming down off the stage road yourself?'

' 'Course I saw 'em!'

'How many would you say were in this bunch?'

'You ever try countin' Injuns in the dark?'

Price considered him a moment. 'What gave you the notion they were Indians?'

'Who else would be ridin' that trail after night? Prob'ly the same murderin' devils that burned out Fenwick. They hit Archer's place, too. Didn't you know that?'

'How many in this bunch?' Price said again.

'Well, I was up on that mesa when they dropped below the bridge an' my eyes ain't what they was twenty years ago. But I'd say upwards of two dozen anyhow—'

'Where's that natural born loud-talking gun boss of yours?'

But, before the girl could answer, Cope came loping up from the herd and said, running hardeyes over Dog Hair, 'What's this duffer want? We ain't runnin' no free lunch.'

Joyce explained the situation and Cope looked at Price. 'I think,' Price said, 'our best bet's to drift the cows into those roughs below Archer's—'

'An' spend the next couple of months ridin' our tails off diggin' them out there? You ain't swallerin' this fool's guff about Injuns, are you?'

'It's probably Flack,' Price nodded, 'but we can't buck him here. We could hold that south pass—'

'We could shout, too,' Cope sneered.

'We can't hold off two dozen men with—'

'Fighting's *my* department.' Cope said to the girl. 'This nizzy old coot able to handle that rifle?'

She nodded and Price said, 'You try fighting them here and you'll have a stampede—'

Joyce said stubbornly, 'I'm not going to be run out of here again.'

'You ain't goin' to be run out,' Cope grinned. 'You an' Price grab a couple of rifles, an' go down to that pass he wants to take the cows through. Archers stuff will roll first. When they heave into sight kill enough to turn 'em back. I'll take care of these range roughers.'

Price, minded to assert his authority, had a

173

hard time keeping his mouth shut. But the reasons he'd had for not crossing Cope before were still bright in his thoughts. So all he finally said was, 'How?'

'Ambush. They're askin' for it an' they'll git it. Only one way to handle that breed of cats. Feed 'em the fear an' you will see their heels pronto.' He said to the cook, 'Call the boys an' let's git started.' He stabbed a finger at Whiskers. 'You're goin' with us an' you'll git paid for it, too. A good Injun fighter is just what the doc ordered.'

They were better than halfway to Spanish 40 before Price opened his mouth. Then he said, 'That "Uncle Jim" pelican is the bird that threw those slugs at us off the mesa that morning we were crossing the bench.'

'I know,' Joyce said wearily. 'He's been working for Fenwick.'

'Kind of rattlebrained type to put any trust in.'

'He's all right. He's had a pretty hard life. His whole family was wiped out by Apaches forty years ago. He was scalped and left for dead himself. Lived on berries and nuts for weeks, they say, and what rabbits he could manage to knock over with a club. He was already here when the cow spreads came in. Rode for several of them when he was younger. When Dad bought the Basin he helped us with the clearing and planting. He's harmless enough—'

174

'He didn't sound very harmless when he was using that rifle.'

Her head came around to him and that way, still watching him, she let her horse drift into a walk. 'And you pride yourself on being practical!'

Price let it ride.

'I know what's biting you,' she said, 'and it's got nothing to do with Uncle Jim. It's the things you've got in your head that won't gee.'

Price, moving his glance through the roundabout shadows, kept his jaw hobbled and refused to be drawn.

'Some people,' Joyce declared harshly, 'are so damn stubborn they wouldn't move camp for a prairie fire!'

'I'll agree with you there.'

'At least I'm willing to face the facts!'

'And what facts am I dodging?'

She said, suddenly angry, 'I should have got someone else. I should have known that first night you were too straight-laced—'

'A man can't do his best fighting in the dark. If you had told me then what you had in your mind—'

'You'd have walked right out on the deal, and I knew it. You don't believe in an eye for an eye. You're the forbearing kind. Like my father.'

'It's a hard world, Sloan, but we've all got to live in it. Two wrongs don't make a—'

'You and your copybook maxims! Half a

175

man's no good to me in this business—'

'What you want is a butcher like Cope.'

'At least he knows how to get the job done and he isn't handicapped by any set of outmoded principles he has to stop and get the best of every time he's faced with an issue!'

'Nope. Not that guy,' Price said grimly. 'And when he's got things whipped into line he'll put the same code of ethics to work on you and take over this place and these cows for himself.'

'He wouldn't dare!'

'A fellow like that will dare anything. Which is why you cotton to him. But you'll see when the time comes. Vengeance belongs to God and when you fly in the face of God, Sloan, you're going to wind up with the short end of the stick.'

'Sometimes you can be just plain insufferable!'

Price grinned. 'Insufferable is a tag folks have got into the habit of putting on—'

He broke off to twist round in the saddle. The wind was on their left sides, still coming off the mountains, but they both heard the sound, of gunfire. 'Come on!' Price scowled, and put spurs to his horse, lifting it into a headlong run.

The girl needed no urging with the thought of those stampeding cattle behind them. Price hoped neither horse would step into a dog hole, yet in a way he was grateful for this need of speed which necessarily put an end to their uncomfortable conversation. He knew that talk couldn't solve what lay between him and Joyce and he was pretty well convinced talk wouldn't turn her from her purpose. She had lived with her hate too long to be changed by words.

And he was right about that. But where a man would have dropped it and been glad to have it dropped, Joyce, when they got into the defile and swung their mounts to face back into the Basin, picked up the thread of their conversation, saying bitterly, 'We may as well thrash this out and face it. My use of hired guns and my determination to get the best of those crooks in that Combine is but the smallest part of why we don't get along. It's *me* you can't get out of your head.'

Price stared into the gloom without speaking.

'I'm not a child, Morg. I know you want me terribly and not just for now, but you don't want me hard enough to quit your damn thinking. And that's not enough—it won't ever be enough. I don't want half a man. I don't want any part of a man who, every time we come together, has a head full of questions and a mind full of wondering how many others have been there before him.'

Even after it was plain he had no intention of answering she waited, trying to make out the shape of his face in the starlight. She was

177

still looking at him, still watching and waiting for whatever he might say, when they caught the first far-off rumble of hoofs.

She took a long breath. 'And so I'm letting you go, Morg. I'm paying you off when we get back to the wagon.'

Price spoke then. He said, 'That's one way of putting it.'

'What do you mean?'

'What difference can it make? You've got your hopes pinned on this leather slapper—'

He broke off, twisting around to stare east with a curse. 'There, by God—there's your answer! We've been gulled!' he cried, pointing.

Joyce, staring into the Basin's churning shadows with the pounding of hoofs building up their wild thunder, saw the front of the herd swing left and go pounding into the east, heading straight for the cut that would take them to Anvil. Her widened eyes saw the wink of muzzle lights; her ears caught the barking of six-shooters, but so wholly unexpected was this change in direction she did not realize the import of what was taking place until Price, yelling to make himself heard, cried, 'That bunch off the stage road was decoys! We've got to reach the Notch ahead of Gill's riders or you've had your last look at those cattle!'

CHAPTER SIXTEEN

Ira Flack, who had started his life as a Coffeyville barkeep in the days of the Daltons, had never watered down his luck with any excess baggage in the scruples department. Strictly a Main Chance man cultivating a Harvard accent behind a tubercular pallor he'd rolled into Quinn's Crossing some eleven years back and proceeded to hitch his wagon to the rising star of Nick Baglio, in whose King Midas Bar he'd started dealing a little faro between the whisky sours.

Nick was a good connection, being head of the mining camp's Vigilance Committee as well as behind-the-scenes overlord of all organized crime in that district. And Flack had known how to make himself useful. So much so that when an acute attack of lead poisoning had shaken Nick loose of his various interests I. Flack had been able, without much of a rumpus, to inherit not only the King Midas but the bulk of the deposed czar's illicit revenues besides.

One thing he hadn't been able to lay hands on was the toast of the diggings, Nick Baglio's protegee, Lily White, the night-blooming cereus whose sweet voice and bright smile had dragged men into the King Midas like flies. Miss Lily, quite a gal in her own right and a lecher's dream incarnate, had genteelly made it known in words of one syllable she needed no man's chest to cry on and no help at all with her personal affairs.

The 'flaming iceberg' Flack had dubbed her when she had taken herself off to set up a rival establishment. Though he'd done everything he could think of short of antagonizing himself with local opinion, he had not been able to close up her place or rid the camp of her. His carefully nurtured smear campaigns had fallen on deaf ears. She was the 'angel' of all and sundry because she hired no strumpets to part men from their wages, would not tolerate crooked dealing and served the best and greatest variety of liquors that could be had anyplace in the Territory. Even now when he recalled her, as he sometimes did when his luck was low, it was with the frustrated malice of knowing she represented the only damned wall he'd never carried by assault.

But this evening, as he strolled about his well-filled tables, inclining occasional nods at familiar faces among the three-deep crush at the bar, he was in fine fettle, his mood more than usually expanded by the comforting reflection that, before another sun got up, he would have 'this goddam country' just about where he wanted it.

He saw his brother come into the place from the street, his black clothes grayly powdered with trail dust; and he paused to fire up a cheroot before following the marshal into the back room. He was still feeling comfortable when he pushed shut the door, but one look at his brother's disgruntled features stretched the skin of his own white and bleak at the creases.

The marshal looked at him and grunted. 'No dice,' he said gruffly.

Flack parked a hip on the near edge of his desk and thoughtfully bumping the lifted heel, watched his brother paw through a curtain draped cupboard. After a moment he got up. Taking a bottle and glass from a drawer he'd pulled out, he said disgustedly, 'Here!' and pushed them over the unlittered top of the desk. 'Price wasn't there, eh?'

'He was there and I saw him and that was the end of it.'

Flack waited till the marshal had splashed the glass full of whisky, had thrown the stuff down his throat and was reaching for more. 'Why didn't you pick up the horse?' he said thinly.

'Because the horse wasn't there—'

'You had a warrant. Why didn't you serve it?'

'The scut threw a cup of scaldin' coffee. While I was duckin' he snatched out his gun. Nothin' I could do but hit the breeze after that, an' I done it. Said if you want to go on breathin' you had better lay off. Because if you don't, he says, he's liable to come in here after you.'

A hard grin curled around the edge of Flack's cigar. 'In about one hour,' he said, looking at his watch, 'he'll be almighty lucky if he's still on his feet. I've sent half the riffraff in town out the stage road—told them they could have anything they can pick up. All they're like to get will be a batch of hot lead; but while they're collecting it,' he said, quietly chuckling, 'Gill's crew will be taking those cows through the Notch.'

The marshal's jowls, going slack, turned a fish-belly white. A scared look jittered across the bulge of his jaw and he was reaching, green of cheek, for the courage in the bottle when the kicked-open door struck the wall with a crash.

The marshal, whirling, jerked spread hands up in front of his face, but Flack's voice bit through the racket to say wickedly, 'You better have good reason for busting, in here like this.'

Joe Archer walked brazenly into the room and his father, on crutches, hobbled bitterly after him. The marshal, looking frantic and mumbling something about his horse, escaped into the barroom before his brother could collar him.

'The best in the world,' Joe told Flack, grinning. 'I'm goin' to hand you Bunchgrass Basin, Ira. All wrapped up an' tied with pink ribbon.'

'I'm allergic to pink,' Flack said, and Joe

182

guffawed.

'You won't pass up this deal.'

The gambler eyed him a moment and went over and shut the door. Returned to his desk he said through the smoke of his refired cheroot, 'No room in my plans for bunch quitters, Archer.' And then, to Joe's father: 'What are you crawling back for?'

The old man, taking his weight on his crutches, stared unfathomably at Flack and said nothing. Joe Archer said, 'We're aimin' to pull out if we can sell Spanish 40. What will you give for the place—stock an' everything?'

'Not interested.'

'You better *git* interested if you want Bunchgrass Basin.'

'I can take it without any help from you.'

'But not legal,' Joe grinned. 'My way you can—'

'Never mind the build-up. Just tick off the facts.'

'How much you offerin' for Spanish 40?'

Flack said without expression, 'I'll give you two thousand dollars—'

'Come on,' Joe told his father, 'the girl will do better than that.'

Flack let them get as far as the door. 'All right. I'll give you seven. Take it or leave it.'

'We'll take it,' Joe said. 'Go dig up your money.'

Flack fetched a paper out of a drawer and placed it on the desk with bottled ink and a pen. 'I'll want a signature to this.' He got a roll of bills from his pocket, counting a small heap of them onto the desk as Joe's dad hobbled forward to pick up the pen. 'Sign right there,' Flack said, pointing, and the old man scratched his name.

Joe picked up the banknotes, riffling the ends of them.

'Now let's hear your proposition.'

'You're goin' to like this,' Joe said and, when he got done talking, the gambler nodded.

He sat silent awhile as though turning it over. Then he picked a wet shred off the butt of his stogie. In the bar outside a sagebrush band swung into the rollicking strains of *Sally Gooden*. 'When are you figuring to leave?' he asked Archer.

Joe said, 'We're not goin' back an' I don't see any reason for waitin' till mornin'. The sooner we shake the dust of this country the better I'll be suited.'

'You're pulling out right away then?'

Eyes narrowing, Joe said, 'We'll leave when we git ready.'

The gambler shrugged. 'Don't let me keep you.' Picking up the bargain-and-sale deed the elder Archer had signed he dropped it into the wide flat drawer above his knees, slyly listening to the thump of the old man's crutches.

The pair were at the door and Joe was reaching for the knob when Flack's hand came above the desk with a pistol. The gun bucked twice and he had just finished cleaning it when the band in the bar wound up its fling with the ubiquitous Sally.

Flack opened the back door and dragged the two bodies out into the alley. Returning, he put the currency Joe had taken back into his bankroll, coolly dusted his hands and fired up a fresh stogie.

CHAPTER SEVENTEEN

Though their horses were enough fresher than those of the men making off with the cattle to allow Price and Joyce to cut around and get ahead of them, they were unable to do this without attracting the raiders' notice. Lead whined and whistled as it went tunneling past them and they were forced to extend their mounts to the utmost to get beyond range of the rustlers' guns.

'How much farther?' Price shouted when the bunch with the cattle finally dropped behind them.

'Not much—not more than a mile. But I can't see how we're to stop them.'

Price couldn't either, but it was the only chance they were likely to get. 'Once they've put that bunch through the mountains you've lost Archer's and probably the bulk of your own. Those fellows know this range a lot better than we do and they'll scatter those critters to hell and gone. How close to the Notch does Flack's spread run?'

The girl's reply was torn away by the wind. They'd been steadily climbing and on these high slopes it had assumed gale proportions. 'I can't hear you,' Price yelled. Joyce spurred nearer, leaning toward him. 'I said my horse is playing out!'

Price slowed his own, peering anxiously backward over his shoulder. The dark mass of the cattle was not half a mile behind. Joyce, cupping a hand about her mouth, shouted, 'It levels off up ahead.' But even at a lope her mount continued to lag and Price let his horse drop into a walk.

'You head for camp,' he told her, but Joyce shook her head at him obstinately.

'You don't know the country. When you get through the Notch you're on Anvil range and it's all broken up with hogbacks and canyons—'

'I'm not going through the Notch.'

'You'll never check that herd by yourself; there isn't anyplace to stop them.'

'Then we'll make a place,' Price said.

'Let them go. I don't want you killed for them. There's one terrible drop partway through where the wall's sheered away on the left—'

'Bad place for the cattle.'

'It could be if they try to run them through.

186

They won't. They've been trying to work the run out of them—'

'They've been trying to catch *us*,' Price said, looking back, 'and they're just about to do it. Kick that crowbait—use your reins on him.'

The girl's mount made the effort but its strength was gone. Its breath was the in-and-out wheeze of a cracked bellows. Great patches of lather gave it the look of a paint and the forward drive of its unwieldy legs held only the promise of imminent collapse. Nothing but an ingrained habit of response, and the immeasurable gameness of a heart that was pounding the guts right out of it, was keeping this cowpony in motion.

'Pull up,' Price growled.

'But Morg, the Notch—'

He followed her pointing hand through the starshine. He saw the deep gash of the pass just ahead—perhaps an eighth of a mile—and knew it might as well have been far off as the moon which, in its first quarter, had not yet come up.

Even as the thought laid its track through his head he caught the blind lurch of the animal's stumble. 'Jump!' he cried harshly; but she was on a dead horse that suddenly fell apart under her.

She'd kicked free of the stirrups and rolled clear as it went down. But the fall had shaken her. She was slow getting up. Price, leaping down, swung her into his saddle. 'Guide the horse,' he panted, and jumped up behind her.

He didn't have to look behind to know the herd was almost on them. He could hear the clack and rattle of that mad sea of horns—the earth-shaking rumble from those hundreds of cloven hoofs. He could hear the shouts of the raiders.

And he saw how the rims of these hills pinched in like the wings of a holding pen, funneling everything into the pass. Price looked back then.

The muzzle lights of exploding belt guns revealed the placement of those harrying riders. They were dropping back, howling like Comanches, and too late Bar O's ramrod understood their purpose. Plain thievery was no longer activating these men; they were bent on destruction, inciting the crazed herd to an even wilder frenzy, striving to bring forth the last full gust of speed of which these terrified brutes were capable—and they were getting it.

No longer had Price or the girl any choice. There was no chance now to swerve and pull out of this—no place to go if Price could turn the horse, even. He had committed the girl to a race against death. The jaws of the hills had caught them, locking them into the black gullet of the pass.

The thunder of the herd was like the roar of an avalanche. Its breath enveloped them in a wild smell of fright. Only scant yards separated those horns from the foam-flecked rump of their over-burdened horse.

Price never touched it but he knew that carrying double it was not going to last this ride out.

He bent his head against the girl's and was not thinking of the cattle. 'How much farther to that bad place?'

'We're coming to it now!'

'And how far, after that, to the end of this slot?'

'About another thirty rods.'

'What happens then?'

'The trail gets wider, opens out. But it still isn't good. It starts down, all tangled up in a maze of—'

'Okay. Let's have my rifle.'

'Morg, you can't—'

'All I want is the rifle'

'But what good can it do? You can't stop them now! We're crossing the ledge-it's barely thirty feet wide and nothing on the left but a straight-down drop! Those cows are being pushed too—'

'Damn it!' Price cried. 'Will you hand me that rifle?'

Her chin lifted angrily but she yanked the repeater out of its scabbard. Price took it.

'Crowd the horse hard against that righthand wall.'

'We can't stop here—'

'No one's asking you to stop! See if you can do what you're told for once, will you?'

189

He felt the horse swerve.

When he felt it straighten out he yelled in her ear, 'Now for Christ's sake don't stop!' and shoved himself backward off the horse's rump.

*   *   *

Uncle Jim, riding north with the Bar O crew, knew a feeling of importance he had seldom achieved before. He was a valued part of a punitive expedition which could never have been launched had he not ridden to warn them.

He touched Cope's sleeve. 'These fellows don't look like redskins; they've got too smart to wear feathers. These days they're got up pretty much like we are. But don't let that fool you.'

'I won't,' Cope assured him. 'You reckon you can find a good place for us to lay for 'em?'

'Sure can,' said Jim, and pointed his mount into the dark swirl of shadows. 'Jest foller me.'

For the next half hour, without talk, Cope and his gunslicks blindly rode in the wake of a Fenwick pony. Several times during the interval they caught fragmentary snatches of the old gent's staggering prowl through memory. This invariably was concerned with 'redskins' and some of the men began shifting nervous glances. A rider next to Cope summed up the general notion when, shaking his head, he growled, 'Crazy as popcorn.' And another hand muttered, 'This nizzy old gaffer wouldn't know skunks from house cats!'

At last the old man pulled up. 'Right here's as good a place as any,' he said, satisfied.

Cope, peering around, could not make out a thing.

'Don't seem like we've come far enough. My idea,' he said, 'is not to jump 'em any nearer to them cattle than we have to. Can't you find some place a little closer to the bench—'

'You told me you wanted a good spot fer a ambush. You ain't goin' to find no better'n what you've got right here.'

Cope twisted his head. 'I don't hear a damn thing.'

'Injuns,' Jim nodded, 'can be God-awful quiet.'

Cope chewed on his lip awhile. He didn't know the country but he knew this creep-and-shoot game from gun to grab it and he was sure in his own mind they hadn't come far enough. He thrust an impatient glance through the roundabout gloom and the more he stared the less he liked it.

He got down and poked around a bit, feeling of the ground. 'Looks like you've got off the trail.'

The old man said with an intolerant snort, 'You don't reckon them red devils sticks to trails, do you?'

Someone back of Cope swore.

191

The gun boss said, 'If they don't stick to a trail how in time do you know they'll come anyplace near here?'

'Don't know it.'

The silence, turned heavy, pulled taut as a bowstring.

Jim said, 'I reckoned you had that all figgered out. But it don't matter. Injuns likes hair. They likes to dandle it from their breech clouts. Why, them varmints kin smell hair jest like a dog noses out a rabbit! I recollect one time—'

Cope, with a curse, sprang into his saddle. 'Which way's that damn bench?'

Old Jim pointed. 'Off there about four mile—'

They didn't wait for the rest of it. They were gone, hellity larrup, tearing off through the dark.

The old man sat his Turkey Track pony, knee crooked about pommel, staring curiously after them. He was still there, still staring, when ten minutes later his ears picked up the sound of distant gunfire.

'Reckon,' he said, lowering boot to stirrup, 'them tenderfoots done caught hell in two languages. Sure don't' pay to ram round when you're up ag'in' Injuns.'

And, shaking his head, he set off for Joyce's camp.

*   *   *

It was near three o'clock when Flack, in his office, heard a fist pound the panels of the door to the bar. 'Who's there?' he said.

'Piggott.'

Flack told him to come in.

Anvil's lean strayman came in with a blast of noise from the bar, closed the door and, coming over, pulled out a chair and straddled it with arms folded under his chin across its back.

'Let's have it,' Flack said, and Slim Piggott grinned. 'It's about over. We lost a mort of them steers but we got Price for you an' I expect, by this time, we've got that damn girl.'

He told Flack how Gill, when they'd started off with the cattle, had caught sight of two riders trying to cut in ahead of them. 'It was the girl an' that tough ramrod she hired from Two Pole Pumpkin. They was figurin' to turn us at the pass but we crowded 'em too close. The girl's horse give out an' Price had to take her up on his. We knew we had 'em then an' chased 'em onto that ledgerock; drove the herd right in after 'em.

'But when they come to that place where the cliff wall's broke away this Price tries to get smart an' drops off the horse with his rifle. He dropped enough of them critters to swing the bulk of the herd. We figured the girl got clear. Gill's huntin' for her now.'

'And where's Price?'

'Down in the bottom of that canyon with the beef.'

'How do you know?'

'Well, cripes, where else could he be? He wasn't on that trail. We come through in back of the herd an' we looked damn sharp, I can tell you. Nope, them cattle carried him over; you don't need to fret no more about him. Gill said to tell you he'll be along with the girl. We just about had her penned when I took off. We dropped her horse an' she sure ain't goin' to get away from the boys afoot.'

'I hope you've got the straight of it,' Flack said, 'but just in case you're mistaken we'll not take any chances. That guy's played hell enough already. You round up a few boys that know how to work a trigger and—'

'If he didn't go over the cliff with them cattle he'll be diggin' for the tules—'

'That kind of thinking is the reason you're still a strayman. Post your guns where they can cover the street; put them back of doors and windows—put a couple on the roofs. Tell them what he looks like. Tell them you've got five hundred for the guy that rubs him out. Then go sit where you can watch the batwings and keep that smokepole handy.'

CHAPTER EIGHTEEN

Price lay back of the tangled shapes of dead cattle on the brink of the drop when Anvil's crew came up through the dust behind the last of the bawling Herefords. Both his rifle and belt gun were empty. He dared not move a muscle when the riders pulled up, not ten feet away, and sat there discussing his probable fate.

'Tried to turn those fool critters an' got sucked over with 'em.'

'No,' Gill said, 'he was putting them over the cliff deliberate, trying to give the girl a chance to pull clear. He couldn't swing the whole bunch—hadn't time to reload. If she had her luck with her she may have got into that brush off east. We'll look.'

'Hold on.' One of the Anvil riders kneed his horse up nearer the edge. Price's heart climbed into his throat when this man's head twisted round and appeared to be looking straight at him. But in the dark and the dust, lying flat like he was behind those piled-up steers, the man couldn't rightly tell what he was staring at. He freed a boot from stirrup, was making ready to swing down when Gill rasped impatiently, 'No use pawin' at that dead meat; if he didn't go over he will be with the girl. Let's get up there and find her.'

195

Price, after waiting long enough to make sure the departing racket included all of them, began gingerly to crawl across that yielding mass of inert flesh, not a pleasant or easy business with one hand clutching a rifle and the slaughterhouse smell coming up from that canyon a grisly reminder of what could happen if he slipped. He tried to close his ears to the piteous bawling of the crippled survivors but the nauseous feeling of guilt stayed with him even though he knew he'd done the only thing possible.

He was shaking in every joint when finally he stood erect with both feet planted on solid rock. He clamped his jaws and tried to bring his jangled nerves under control. Joyce, even if she had gotten clear, would be in desperate straits because she would almost certainly have pulled aside at the earliest opportunity. Which meant, as Gill had guessed, that she would probably be holed up in the brush not more than a quarter of a mile from here.

The sound of a shot jerked Price erect. He heard a scattering of others and sudden shouts from Gill's crew confirmed his fear that Joyce had been sighted.

He broke into a run, his exhaustion forgotten. Just as he came out of the slot's eastern end he remembered the useless condition of his weapons and belatedly discovered he had no cartridges for the rifle. The trail here dipped downward and was broken and crisscrossed with hogbacks and gullies. Off to the right in the blackness he could hear brush breaking and he let go of the rifle and ran that way, feverishly punching exploded shells from his pistol. He was still too far off, stumbling through the gloom, when he heard the girl scream and knew by Gill's shout they had caught her.

*   *   *

How long he attempted to follow them afoot he was never afterwards able to recall, but he was back on the trail about a mile below the pass with the last rumor of their travel long faded in the darkness when he caught the faint plopping of hoof sound behind him.

It pulled the chin off his chest and yanked all slack from his nerve ends, galvanizing him at once into a dangerous man. Dark and still he coolly stood in the starlight, translating sound into knowledge; and then, quietly, he stepped back into the brush and drew the gun from his holster. Whoever this was, he meant to have that horse.

The rider's descent from the gulch was agonizingly deliberate; but though sweat made a dry nettle-prickling on his cheeks Price kept his place, grimly patient. And then he saw the rider's shape and his hands began to sweat, excitement rushing all through him.

'Uncle Jim!' he called, and the man's hatless

head swung toward him, peering, as conditioned reflex lifted the rifle he'd been riding across the hornless pommel of his McClellan. 'It's Price—Joyce Darling's range boss.'

He stepped into the trail, putting away his pistol, and the old man after a considerable inspection lowered the Winchester's muzzle. 'What in thunder you doin' out here, boy? I dang near mistook—'

'Flack's crowd have grabbed Joyce—'

'You mean Geronimo's, don't you? Them dratted Injuns—'

'Not this time. It was Flack's crew from Anvil. Jack Gill, Flack's foreman, was with them.' He sketched in the events leading up to Joyce's capture. 'I've got to have that horse, Jim.'

The old man climbed down without argument. But handing Price the reins, he said, 'I think you've got Ira Flack all wrong, boy. He might be up to some cussedness but he wouldn't dast lay hands on a nice girl like—'

'What happened to Cope and the crew that went with you?'

'Expect by now they're bein' fitted fer halos. That feller wouldn't hark to me an' run smack into them dratted Injuns.'

Price considered a moment. 'What time's the eastbound stage due in Sunflower?'

' 'Round four o'clock—that'll be,' Jim reckoned, taking a squint at the stars, 'in about one hour. They won't be takin' her there.'

'You might hike over to Anvil on the off-chance I'm wrong, but that girl's in a tight spot, Jim—a mighty tight one. Flack's turned wolf and is too deep in this thing to let a couple more killings get in the way of what he's after.'

*   *   *

Piggott picked up five men who weren't averse to throwing lead, told them what the target looked like and, promising two hundred dollars to the one who scored a bulls-eye, dropped the first man off in the shadows by the bake shop. The second he posted on the roof of the hardware and left another across the way in the blackness of an alley. The fourth he sent to the porch of the Mercantile and cached the fifth behind the Orrison's front door. Then he repaired to the bar.

Custom was beginning to thin out. All but one of the aprons had gone off duty and there weren't but three men with boots on the rail. One of these was the marshal, who had become so immune he'd poured his whiskey on the mahogany and was hoisting an empty glass. There were still a couple of watchers sweating a deal at the faro layout, but it was the only game in progress. And the swamper had come in and was already starting to rack up the chairs.

Piggott slouched to a far corner and, tilting a chair back, staked out his face behind a weeks-old copy of the Phoenix *Republic*. He had worked through the sports, chucked a glance at the ladies' underwear drawings and was yawningly about to take a look at the obits when the batwings skreaked and a girl came angrily in off the street swiftly followed by Gill and the pug-faced Sparks.

The girl, spinning around, tried to regain the doors but the broad shape and spread arms of the burly Sparks blocked her; and Gill, twisting a wrist behind her back, forcibly propelled her in the direction of the office.

You could tell by her look how much force the guy was using but she wasn't being handled without attracting some notice. At the faro layout one man wheeled completely around and, with his cheeks growing dark, asked, 'What's coming off here?'

Gill said, 'Family trouble. You keep outa—'

'That's a lie!' Joyce cried hotly, and tried to twist from his grip. But the Texan piled on pressure and she went nearly to her knees, closing her eyes to hold the tears back. The man by the faro table reached toward his belt but let the hand fall away when he saw Sparks' gun pointed at him.

Letting go of the girl's arm Gill shoved her toward the office and at that precise moment its doorknob was twisted and Flack, suddenly appearing in his black gambler's clothes, stood incredulously staring.

Piggott's ears were still functioning but his mind was caught up in the drama before him and not even the explosion of the marshal's dropped glass could haul his look away from it.

The girl shook back her red hair. She rubbed at the marks of Gill's hand on her wrist and said scornfully to Flack, 'You needn't play act for me.'

Flack, though badly shaken, was coming out if it rapidly. 'What are you doing in Sunflower girl?' He made it sound like a crime and, catching sight of Gill, of Sparks with that naked gun in his fist, became aware of the watching audience: 'Never mind,' he said gruffly. 'This is a clean town, Joyce—you can't ply your trade here.'

'That was always your long suit, wasn't it, Ira? Covering up at the expense of oth—'

'There's a stage due in,' Flack said to Gill, 'and when it leaves I want you to see that she's on it.'

The man who had started to jump Gill said: 'We've had enough of your high-handed stuff around here. This town is getting a little tired, Flack—'

'You want to see it filled up with whores and painted floozies?'

'Those are harsh words, Flack, to fling at a woman.'

'You fool,' Flack snarled, 'this woman is *Joyce Darling*!'

201

'Seems to me there was a Darling used to own Bunchgrass Basin—'

'I know nothing of that, but I tell you straight out you're looking at the strumpet who parlayed a smile and a pair of twisty hips into the worst string of honkeytonks the West has ever known!' Flack's voice shook with fury. 'You let this strip—'

His jaw dropped. His eyes bugged out like knots on a stick and Piggott, suddenly minded of why he'd been sitting there, saw Hi Henry, the stage driver, heave into view scarcely inches away behind the lifting snout of a sawed-off shotgun. Piggott goggled stupidly and then his eyes, bright with fright, picked up the face of Morgan Price.

Flack's hand went blurring hipward. The girl dropped flat against the boards of the floor and faro was forgotten as men dived every whichway. Powder flares pushed smoke rings away from Price's belted middle. Lamp flames danced in the pounding concussions and the marshal collapsed against the front of the bar.

Piggott sprang out of his chair yelling wildly, throwing two shots across the room at Price's shape. The whole place rocked in a blast from the Greener. Flack fell. Something smashed Piggott's teeth and he swayed, coughing blood, and saw Gill through a haze trying to crawl toward the batwings with the whole top half of his face shot away.

Sparks, with both hands thrust above his

hat, stood white as chalk where this fight had caught him; and when a bunch from outside shoved apart the swinging doors he said in ghastly imitation of his usual loud-mouthed manner, 'We got a new deal here, boys. Bar O is goin' to shapin' local politics hereafter an' them as doesn't like it better be huntin' other parts.'

*   *   *

'Sparks was right about one thing,' Joyce said afterwards to Price. 'This country's going to be different. We're all going to pull together and there'll be no more guns carried on this range.'

They were standing in front of the Copper State Livery. Price said, 'Sounds all right if you can make it stick.'

Joyce's lips tightened slightly. 'You're not quitting me, are you?'

'I thought you were going to pay me off—'

'But I can't! All the cash I had left went into those cattle. I was bluffing Sparks' crew; I've been bluffing Cope's gun hands. I've been scraping the barrel's bottom—that's why I didn't buy more grub, Morg. But I've still got that grass and whatever's left of those Herefords . . .'

He looked down at the expressive mouth, at the disturbed and questioning eyes staring up at him; and she, imagining his thoughts were prowling Flack's words, said: 'I did sing in

203

honkeytonks. I owned a couple of gambling halls—'

'I been figuring we'd start over.'

'You mean . . . you *still* want me, Morg?'

'Listen, Strawberry Roan,' Price said, tousling her hair—'why else do you think I've been sticking around?'

LIBRARY & INFORMATION